A PERFECT ARRANGEMENT

'You'd suit me very well. You're tidy, you're intelligent, you're unlikely to vamp me . . . and you can type!' Hardly the most flattering description Holly had ever heard — but for all Ethan Yorke's arrogance — his job offer *was* tempting. And plain Holly, in her business suits and glasses, knew that she was safe . . . Ethan would never look twice at her! So why did she have to go and do a foolish thing like falling in love with him?

Books by Kay Gregory
in the Linford Romance Library:

KAY GREGORY

A PERFECT ARRANGEMENT

Complete and Unabridged

LINFORD
Leicester

First published in Great Britain in 1994

First Linford Edition
published 2012

British Library CIP Data

Gregory, Kay.
   A perfect arrangement. - -
(Linford romance library)
1. Love stories.
2. Large type books.
I. Title II. Series
813.5′4–dc23

ISBN 978–1–4448–1143–8

Published by
F. A. Thorpe (Publishing)
Anstey, Leicestershire

Set by Words & Graphics Ltd.
Anstey, Leicestershire
Printed and bound in Great Britain by
T. J. International Ltd., Padstow, Cornwall

This book is printed on acid-free paper

1

Ethan Yorke stalked into the head office of Smart and Yorke Limited and exhaled a brief sigh of relief. At six o'clock on Christmas Eve he had half expected to find the building deserted.

Fortunately for his purposes, it wasn't.

A nondescript figure, female, and dressed in business navy, sat hunched over a keyboard in the payroll office, punching in data with vigorous application to the task. She was obviously more than competent with a computer, and her short, unadorned fingers were practically flying.

Ethan threw his briefcase on to a desk, and the woman jumped.

'Don't worry,' he drawled. 'I'm not a prowler. I came in quite legitimately through the door.'

The small, stooped figure straightened and turned slowly to face him.

Early twenties, he decided. Ordinary. Straight hair that was neither light nor dark, short nor long. It hung like a faded curtain around her face — a face which made little impression because it was dominated by a pair of oversized tortoiseshell glasses.

Good. Just what he needed. A woman who didn't appear to have pressing social engagements, was probably half intelligent, and shouldn't object to finishing a few odd jobs for him just because it happened to be Christmas Eve.

The wide, unusual golden eyes that he now saw lurked behind the glasses regarded him with pensive concentration.

'I didn't think you were a prowler,' she told him, in a low, surprisingly attractive voice. 'Although the possibility of Marley's ghost did cross my mind.'

Ethan mentally revised his previous stereotyped impression. The woman was also reasonably articulate. 'Really?'

he said. 'I'd never have taken you for Scrooge, Miss . . . ?'

'Adams, Holly Adams.'

'Miss Adams. Am I to understand, then, that you're suffering from a miserly conscience?'

She shook her head, apparently unperturbed by the question, which he had asked more because he imagined some response was expected of him than because he cared.

'No. But it is Christmas Eve, and I'm working late in my office. The connection was hard to avoid.'

'And your name is Holly. Even more appropriate.'

'It should be. I was born on Christmas Day. And I have a twin brother — '

'Whose name, of course, is Noel.' Ethan made a conscious effort not to sound nauseated, and he knew he had succeeded when, for the first time since he'd entered the office, he saw the woman's pale, unpainted lips part in a rather sweet smile.

'How did you guess?' she murmured.

'I have unusually acute deductive powers,' he replied drily.

'And a swollen head too, I think. Is there something you're looking for, Mr Yorke, or did you just drop in to check out the corridors of power?'

Ethan's eyes narrowed. 'Hardly. I've been familiar with this building all my life. There aren't any corridors left for me to check. How did you know who I am?'

'Your picture has joined your father's and Mr Smart's on the boardroom wall.'

'Has it, now? How very curious.'

'I don't see why.' Holly, frowning, reminded him of a myopic mother owl.

'Don't you? Because I haven't sat for a portrait in years, that's why.' He hitched a hip on the edge of the nearest desk and wondered why he had troubled to explain.

'Oh, I see. Yes, you look much younger and more approachable in your picture,' she said candidly. 'You've been

4

in Canada, haven't you?'

'Yes,' he snapped, irritated that this uninspiring young woman had had the nerve to call him not only swollen-headed but unapproachable.

No doubt the whole of the London office knew his history, but he had no intention of discussing it with Holly Adams, an odd little lump of a girl who was looking at him as if he were some kind of specimen in a lab.

He remembered the last time he had become aware that the entire staff was staring at him with that particular expression in their eyes. It was when he had fallen so besottedly for Alice. They had all known it — and guessed also that he was being taken for a fool. He shrugged and flicked a sliver of silver tinsel off his sleeve. He had been young and impulsive in those days. Now he was older and a lot wiser — and he had his hormones well under control.

But he was wasting time. He glanced at his watch. Ten past six, and he was picking Diane up at eight.

'Miss Adams,' he said briskly, 'I've been working on some figures since I got back. I'd like you to enter them for me and run a print-out so I can finish the job over Christmas. I'll need it by seven-thirty at the latest.'

Holly didn't answer him at once, but when she did it was to remark mildly, 'I'm assistant to the payroll manager, Mr Yorke.'

'Who is responsible to me, Miss Adams. I fail to see the problem.'

She opened her mouth, seemed about to say something, but then appeared to change her mind.

Without further ado, Ethan snapped open his briefcase and pulled out a sheaf of papers. 'Here you are,' he said. 'Get on with these right away, if you don't mind.'

Holly Adams took the papers without a word, but as he turned away he thought he heard a voice mutter, 'And if I do mind you don't give a damn.'

He swung around quickly, but she had her back to him and was busy

6

putting his papers in order. He thought of reminding her of who was boss by telling her not to be impertinent, but decided to put it off until later. Right now it was more important to him that she get on with the job. He could do it himself if he had to, but data entry wasn't a chore he enjoyed. Besides, she was right. He didn't especially give a damn. Employees were employees. To be treated with reasonable courtesy and kept at an impersonal distance. He had learned that lesson the hard way. Holly Adams had nothing better to do on Christmas Eve or she wouldn't be here, and, as the new president, it was entirely up to him whose work she did.

Flicking another strand of tinsel off his lapel, he strolled into the payroll manager's office and made a mental note to tell Cliff Haslett to add overtime to Miss Adams's December pay-cheque. Then he picked up the phone to call Diane.

* * *

Holly slammed her desk drawer shut and stamped past the pink Christmas tree with an expression of such ferocity on her round and normally placid face that her friends would scarcely have recognised her.

How dared that arrogant, dictatorial man walk into her office on Christmas Eve and demand that she drop everything for him? He hadn't even realised he was imposing. She was an employee of Smart and Yorke, and as far as he was concerned that meant she was also his slave.

She stepped into the lift, and watched the doors close slowly, blotting out the tree and its decorations.

Humbug indeed, she thought viciously. And Ethan Yorke had had the nerve to ask her if *she* had a miserly conscience.

It's your own fault, Holly, murmured a small, annoying voice in her brain. You could perfectly well have told him that your sister-in-law expected you home by seven, and that you had only stayed late because you wanted to get a head start on month-end work — not act as skivvy to some god in the executive office. She sighed. A god who just happened to be president.

Scowling, she marched across the spacious front lobby, knowing full well she hadn't told him any of those things because she liked her job and wanted to keep it. It was bad enough that she hadn't been able to resist that crack about his swollen head and the corridors of power. He hadn't liked it, she knew. But that air of being totally in charge of his world had rubbed her the wrong way from the moment he'd walked into the office. And she hadn't liked his autocratic attitude. Arrogant executive despot!

By the time she arrived at the unpretentious house in Chiswick where she rented a room from her brother and his wife, Holly felt like Scrooge and the Grinch rolled up in one. She was also ready to consign Smart and Yorke's very successful ladies' wear chain, which had Canadian and Australian outlets as well, to the bottom of the North Atlantic. Along with the new president. *Especially* the new president.

She unlocked the front door and realised she was, quite literally, grinding her teeth.

Noel, who was crossing the hall, stopped at once. 'Merry . . . ' His voice trailed into silence as his startled gaze fell on Holly's face.

'Merry Christmas Eve,' replied Holly, still grinding.

Noel took her arm and pulled her quickly inside. 'Barbara, I'm getting a drink for Holly,' he called, dodging round two fat black cats as he led his sister into a warm, old-fashioned kitchen with gingham curtains on rings and hand-painted yellow wooden cupboards. He sat her down at an oilcloth-covered table that took up the centre of the room. 'She looks as if she needs it.'

Barbara stopped what she was doing at the stove, and turned to stare. 'What's the matter?' she asked worriedly. 'Don't tell me *you're* coming

10

apart, Holly. You never do.'

It wasn't true, but Holly could see why her dark-eyed, beautiful sister-in-law might think so. She had long ago learned to conceal her hurts, keep smiling, and make the best of what life had to give her. Short, slightly overweight women with round, indistinct features and poor eyesight needed to emphasise their competent good humour and helpfulness, not fall apart at the drop of a hat. She would have enjoyed throwing a tantrum at Ethan Yorke, though, she decided grimly. He could do with a good shaking up . . .

Her eyes glazed over, and she no longer saw the cluttered kitchen with its heap of unwashed dishes on the counter and the soft balls of cat fuzz on the floor.

Instead she was remembering Ethan Yorke as he had looked when she told him she worked for Mr Haslett — as if she were a company robot who had had the temerity to answer him back.

Probably his good looks had conditioned him to expect instant acquiescence from the female sex.

Not that he was unusually tall, as she recollected, but he was powerfully built, and although his uneven features were by no means classically handsome, their arrangement was undeniably sensual. And then there was that wonderfully glossy brown hair, thick and curling up at his neck. His eyes were brown too, deep and heavy-lidded. It wasn't hard to imagine that those eyes, along with strong cheekbones, and quite extraordinarily full and sensual lips, would make a great many women regard him as the catch of the season. In fact he was the sort of man who rarely noticed women like Holly existed — except to type. As his sort was invariably also inconsiderate, self-centred and autocratic, she had never felt that was much of a loss.

'Holly? I said what's the matter. If you want to talk you'd better get on with it before Chris comes home from next door.'

Her sister-in-law's voice brought Holly back to her surroundings. Barbara was right. Her three-year-old nephew was his aunt's greatest fan and admirer, but she knew from experience that coherent conversation would cease the moment he returned.

'It's our new president,' she explained to Barbara. 'Colby Yorke has decided to retire and hand over the London operation to his son.'

'Oh. I thought you said the son was running things in Canada.'

'He was. For ten gloriously peaceful years. Ever since Edward Smart died.'

Barbara shot her a keen glance and said briefly, 'Explain. What's wrong with the new Mr Yorke?'

Noel appeared with her drink then, so Holly told them both, in Technicolor detail, exactly what was wrong with Ethan Yorke.

'Oh, dear,' said Barbara when she'd finished. 'Was he very intimidating?'

'No. Just arrogant, dictatorial and rude.'

Barbara grinned. 'A good candidate for my mother's sardine and kiwi-fruit stew. She just sent over another pot.'

Holly giggled. 'I'll feed him a double portion.'

Barbara's mother's experimental cooking was regarded by her family as a sure cure for unwanted guests.

'Why didn't you just tell him to stuff it?' demanded Noel, his black beard bristling fraternally.

Holly shrugged. 'I suppose because that's not what I do.'

'Quite right,' said Barbara soothingly. 'Now, then — it's Christmas. Let's forget about work, and especially about Holly's new boss. He probably won't bother her again.'

It was good advice, Holly was obliged to acknowledge.

Except that she couldn't quite forget about Mr Yorke. He was like a bur that got under the skin, and, although she wasn't quite sure why, she had a feeling he *would* bother her again.

In that, unfortunately, she was right.

Christmas passed pleasantly enough, just as it always had in the days when Holly's parents were alive. But she hadn't been back in the office for more than a few minutes on the Monday following the holiday before Ethan Yorke strode into payroll department and proceeded to set her teeth on edge.

'Miss Adams,' he said coming up behind her just as she sat down at her desk. 'About the work you did for me . . . '

'Yes?' Instead of looking up, Holly picked up a manila folder and began to shuffle pointedly through its contents. 'I hope everything was satisfactory, Mr Yorke.'

'Yes, very. There are just a few changes I'll want made.'

Holly felt her blood rising to a boil. Didn't the man have a secretary? Oh. No, he didn't. She remembered now. Miss Lovejoy in Personnel was interviewing applicants today. All the same, there was a perfectly competent typing pool one floor down. She thought about

15

pointing this out to him, then decided not to. In a way, his request for help was a compliment. Except that it was hardly a request.

He was already placing the papers in front of her and stabbing a strong, square-tipped index finger at the places where he wanted changes made.

'Yes, Mr Yorke. Certainly, just as you say,' said Holly.

Oh, dear. She hadn't intended to adopt that sarcastic, phonily obsequious tone with him, but somehow that was how it came out.

If Ethan Yorke noticed the sarcasm, he didn't comment, but continued to issue clipped and precise instructions as if he were dictating notes to a machine. Which was precisely how he regarded her, of course.

She folded her lips together, took the papers, and told him she would try to have the work ready by half-past eleven.

'Eleven,' he said. 'You can manage that, I imagine.'

'Yes, if I don't answer the phone,

ignore Mr Haslett's memo, and skip my coffee break,' replied Holly, tapping a pencil on her desk.

'Good. Do that.'

She was just opening her mouth to respond when she realised he was already on his way to the door.

She half turned in her chair and was irritated to see the eyes of every woman in the department fixed surreptitiously on the movement of his muscular body as he crossed the room. The elegant cut of a dark grey suit only served to accentuate his potent appeal.

Pushing her glasses viciously up her nose, Holly turned back to her keyboard and began to pound at it as if that athletic body lay at the mercy of her fingers — and not in any pleasurable sense either, she thought furiously, as visions of a suitably pounded president passed improbably but satisfactorily through her head.

She finished the changes at eleven o'clock on the dot and looked up, half expecting to see the president erupting into the department to demand what had taken her so long. But there was no sign of him. She wondered if she was expected to deliver the work to his office in person. Yes, presumably she was. The mountain might have come to the minion once, but that didn't mean he meant to do it again.

She stood up and made her way to the lift.

The presidential office was on the tenth floor. Holly had never been near it, but she expected to pass through an outer office fiercely guarded by a dragon at a desk. Indeed the desk was there, as expected, equipped with in- and out-trays, executive blotter and pens. But the dragon was missing.

She paused, staring doubtfully at the door to the inner sanctum. Its brass nameplate read, 'Ethan J. Yorke.' She wondered vaguely what the J stood for. Jaws, she decided, as she lifted her hand to knock lightly.

'Yes, Miss Lovejoy?' a clipped voice rapped from within. 'Tell her to wait.'

'I'm not Miss Lovejoy,' said Holly.

'What?' There was silence for a moment, followed by the sound of a drawer slamming shut. Then the door was whipped open. Holly felt its wind on her face.

'Oh,' said Ethan J. Yorke. 'It's you. Why didn't you say so? I was expecting Miss Lovejoy with another brain-dead female who thinks long legs and a neat backside are all the qualifications she needs for the job.' He shook his head. 'And Lovejoy tells me those are the pick of the crop.'

'Really?' said Holly, surprising herself. 'Are you saying that any woman who looks halfway attractive must also be brain-dead? That's a very old-fashioned attitude Mr Yorke.'

'I'm an old-fashioned man. Chauvinistic too, if that's what you were about to say next.' He ran his eyes briefly over her brown suit and clean but unremarkable face. 'You don't appear to waste your time adorning the lily, Miss Adams.'

Ridiculously, Holly felt something inside her shrivel up. She had long ago come to terms with the fact that men valued her mainly for her cheerful efficiency and good nature, so why did she suddenly feel crushed because Mr Yorke had rudely stated the obvious?

'As you say, it would be a waste of time,' she replied.

He pushed a hand through his thick brown hair, and sighed. Impatiently. 'That was tactless of me, wasn't it?' He made it sound as though his lack of tact were her fault.

Holly tried to smile, but couldn't quite manage it. 'Not at all. It's true I don't bother much with make-up. Here are your print-outs, Mr Yorke.'

'Hmm.' He took the bulky folder from her without looking at it, and she saw him glance over her shoulder. 'Ah. I see Miss Lovejoy approaching with a fresh set of legs in tow.'

Holly saw his eyes narrow in speculation, but she resisted the urge to turn and stare. 'In that case I'll leave you to enjoy them,' she said, again surprised to hear the caustic note in her voice.

For a moment Ethan Yorke looked surprised too, but he only said curtly, 'Thank you, Miss Adams. That will be all.'

As Holly headed back to the lift, she passed Miss Lovejoy, looking slightly frazzled, and a tall, dark young woman with perfect teeth.

I hope she buries them in his throat, thought Holly uncharitably. The more she saw of the new Mr Yorke, the less she liked him.

For the rest of the day she succeeded in putting him out of her mind. She had lost enough time through his interruptions, and she wasn't about to lose any more. Luckily he was seven floors above her and out of sight — no doubt perusing more of Miss Lovejoy's leggy applicants.

At five o'clock, just as she was clearing her desk, Mr Haslett, the payroll manager, lumbered over to her small glassed-in office.

Mr Haslett was a large barrel of a man with a rolling gait and the face of a sad-eyed clown. He looked sadder than ever this evening.

'Mr Yorke wants to see you, Holly,' he said sepulchrally. 'I just had a chat with him on the phone. Young Mr Yorke, I mean. It's official now that Mr Yorke senior has finally detached himself from the business and gone to golf.'

'Oh,' said Holly, glancing at her watch. 'I was just getting ready to go home.'

'Sorry.' Mr Haslett looked as if he meant it. 'Can't be done. I don't know him well, but I understand young Mr Yorke isn't a man who takes kindly to being crossed. If he wants to see you now, you'd better go. Besides . . . ' he looked even gloomier ' . . . I gather it may be to your advantage.'

Holly didn't see how missing her train was likely to be to her advantage, but she supposed she hadn't much choice. Mr Yorke was the boss, she was the employee, and if he said 'Jump' — or in this case 'Take the lift' — she'd better do it or start seeking alternative employment. This reflection didn't do a thing to ease her mind. Nor did it improve her opinion of the man as she stood in the lift bearing her up to the celestial heights of the presidential suite.

She noted that there was still no dragon guarding the door.

'Come in,' snapped the voice that was becoming all too familiar. 'Don't just stand there.'

Lord, he was getting worse. He was bad enough at the beginning of a promising day, impossible at the end of a bad one.

'I said come in,' he repeated when Holly didn't respond at once.

She went in.

He was leaning back in his chair behind an enormous executive desk which took up a quarter of the roomy, white-carpeted office. At an angle through the main window Holly could glimpse the dome of St Paul's.

'Ah. Miss Adams.' He gave her a smile which reminded her of a wolf licking its lips in anticipation of a particularly succulent lunch. 'That was an excellent job you did for me.'

'Thank you,' said Holly stiffly, wondering if he had made her miss her train just to tell her what she already knew.

'Mmm.' He pressed his fingertips together and continued to regard her with a pensive, thoroughly disconcerting stare. 'You've been with Smart and Yorke for some years, haven't you?'

'Five. I came here straight from school.'

'Which would put you around twenty-three. You've worked your way up the company ladder remarkably quickly. Are you ambitious, Miss Adams?'

Holly frowned. 'I don't know. Maybe. I haven't thought about it. I'm not angling for Mr Haslett's job, if that's what you mean.'

'Just as well, as I'm not offering it to you. Sit down.' He picked up a pencil and waved it at a black chair in front of his desk. It looked expensive but none too comfortable.

Holly hesitated a fraction longer than necessary, and he said impatiently, 'I said sit down. It's all right, I haven't electrified the seat.'

'I didn't imagine you had,' she replied, nettled that he had put her hesitation down to her nervousness rather than to a perfectly healthy suspicion that he was about to load her up with more work. But she took the chair he indicated and leaned back, crossing one knee over the other in the hope that he would see her casual demeanour as proof that she didn't lack confidence.

What he actually saw, she realised at once, was the shapely outline of her neat, but sensibly stockinged extremities. Her legs, she knew, were not unattractive, but she rarely drew attention to them, because parading her assets just wasn't her style.

She remembered Mr Yorke's implication that nice legs failed to impress him, so she extended her right one deliberately, and examined the tip of her shoe.

When she looked up, she saw that he was smiling, not ferally now, but with genuine amusement. 'And to think I called you up here partly because I had the fond notion that I wouldn't be presented with more body parts.' He shook his head disbelievingly. 'Very pretty, incidentally, Miss Adams.'

'Thank you,' replied Holly, adding even more starch to her voice.

Ethan Yorke's smile broadened. It was an attractive smile, she supposed, except that she knew better than to be attracted to this kind of man.

'Never mind,' he said. 'In view of your other attributes, I think I can manage to overlook that slight disadvantage. How would you like to work for me, Miss Adams?'

'I already do work for you,' said Holly, mystified.

He put the pencil down and leaned towards her with his fists linked together on the desk. 'I meant for me personally,' he explained. 'As my assistant.'

2

Holly's mouth fell open. She shut it again quickly as thoughts began to tumble around in her mind like jangling marbles.

Was he serious? Or was this his warped idea of a joke? And if he *was* serious, what on earth was she supposed to reply? She didn't want to work any closer to this man than she had to. He would be a hard taskmaster, and a perfectionist with no comprehension that she was a human being with a life of her own. Besides, she liked working for kind Mr Haslett and she liked being assistant manager of Payroll.

'I don't think . . . ' she began, running her tongue over her upper lip. 'I don't think . . . ' She ground to a halt, not knowing what to say next.

'I take it,' said Ethan Yorke in a dry-as-dust voice, 'that the prospect doesn't thrill you. How refreshing.'

Holly stared at him, noting the way a corner of his top lip had tipped up. 'I don't understand,' she said flatly.

'No, I don't suppose you do. The truth is, I've seen enough of Lovejoy's hopefuls. No doubt they're competent enough, but I haven't time for women who insist on flaunting their more obvious attributes around my office. You don't do that.'

She wondered if he meant that there was no danger of her flaunting her attributes because she didn't have any. Except for the legs, which he was willing to overlook. Generous of him, she thought bitterly. And anyway, what did he have against women who made an effort to make the best of themselves? The only reason she didn't trouble much with her own looks was that fussing with her face in front of a mirror just wasn't her idea of recreation. Reading, walking and going out with friends was.

'I don't think you're being fair to the

other applicants,' she said frigidly. 'And I'm sure I wouldn't suit you at all.'

'You'd suit me very well. You're tidy, you're intelligent, you're unlikely to vamp me . . . and you can type!'

Holly began to get the picture. He wanted an insignificant but efficient little nobody who would rush to do his bidding, run errands without attracting attention, and in general act as his Girl Friday and underpaid drudge. And the fact that she hadn't leaped at the chance was cause for more amusement than resentment. He didn't really believe she would turn him down.

'You don't actually want an assistant, do you?' she said. 'You want a full-time slave.'

The eyes that had been fastened on her with detached speculation now turned dauntingly blank. 'Have I given you that impression?' he enquired.

'To be honest, yes.' Holly wasn't sure where she'd found the courage to tell him the truth, but now that she had she couldn't stop. 'You kept me late on

Christmas Eve without even asking if I minded, and today, when I was up to my ears in month-end payroll, you told me to drop everything I was doing because you wanted your work finished. How do you think the staff will take it if their pay-cheques aren't ready on time?'

'But they will be, won't they?' His gaze rested on her with infuriating assurance and more than a little amusement.

'Of course they will. Because if I have to, I'll stay late just to make sure of it.'

'Precisely. That's why I want you, my dear Miss Adams. You're conscientious. If I give you a job to do, you'll do it. Effectively.'

Holly took a deep breath and wondered why the compliment failed to please her. 'Yes. You're quite right. If I took the job I *would* see to it that your work was done properly. But you don't really need an assistant, do you? You need a secretary, and my background happens to be accounting.'

'Yes.' He sat back and looked her

over as if he were the chairman of a negotiating team carefully debating his options. 'I'm aware of your background, Miss Adams, and, as a lot of my work involves figures, I see it as something of an advantage. As to whether you want to call yourself my assistant or my secretary, that's up to you. Either way you'll be adequately paid.'

'Adequately for a secretary,' said Holly.

'I'd say so.' He named a figure. 'Am I correct in thinking that would meet your needs?'

Holly tried not to gasp. Meet her needs! Compared to what she was making now, it was a fortune. 'Yes,' she admitted in a low voice. 'I think it would.'

'Good.' He stood up and planted his hands squarely on the desk. When he bent towards her, she caught the faint, subtle scent of spice, and she saw narrow lines fanning out from the corners of his eyes. He was older than she'd thought, she realised. But of course after spending ten years in Canada he couldn't be much less than thirty-two.

'That's settled, then,' he said, his hard brown gaze pinning her to the back of the chair. 'I've already informed Cliff Haslett. Until he's had time to train your replacement you will spend mornings with me and afternoons in Payroll. In a couple of weeks I'll expect you up here full-time.'

'But . . . ' Holly swallowed. 'Mr Yorke, I haven't decided — '

'You don't have to. I've decided. However, if you have any doubts, naturally you'll be on trial for the first month.' He smiled, but it was a cynical sort of smile that didn't do a lot to soothe her nerves. 'I suppose, of necessity, that means I will also be on trial. You may rest assured I won't demand services that might be classified as beyond the call of duty.'

There was a provocative note in his deep voice now, and Holly felt sure he wanted to see if she would blush. She almost did, but with annoyance, not with embarrassment.

'I didn't imagine you planned to chase me around the desk,' she replied coldly. 'Very well, Mr Yorke. I'm willing to try it for a month.'

For that amount of money she'd be a fool not to. After all, she had given up her flat and moved in with her brother and his wife because they were having trouble making mortgage payments on Noel's less than generous commission as a car salesman. The rent she paid enabled them to keep their heads above water.

Holly closed her eyes briefly. Mr Yorke's astonishing salary offer meant that she would be able to help her family even more. It also meant she could save something towards the purchase of a small place of her own in a few years' time. It was the beginning of a dream come true.

She lifted her head, meeting the president's narrowed gaze boldly. 'As far as services are concerned, I will do anything that falls within the job description,' she informed him. 'Miss Lovejoy showed it to me.'

'Really? What point are you making, Miss Adams?' He bent closer so that she could see the five o'clock shadow darkening his jaw. There was a disconcerting glitter in his eyes.

'That my job will not include making tea or coffee, taking your suits to the cleaners, or buying gifts for your wife,' replied Holly, leaning as far away from him as she could.

She didn't really mind making coffee, and taking his suits to the cleaners or buying gifts could very well prove a welcome break from routine. But he had raised her hackles with that unnecessary gibe.

She watched him straighten slowly and stand with his hands behind his back.

'I don't have a wife,' he said distantly, 'so that doesn't enter into it. As for making coffee and delivering suits

— well, we'll see. Thank you, Miss Adams, I don't think I need keep you any longer. I'll expect you at nine o'clock. Sharp.'

Holly entertained a moment's charming fantasy of arriving in his office at nine o'clock armed with a dagger. Sharp. But she only nodded non-committally, said, 'Yes. Goodnight Mr Yorke,' and departed for the enclosing privacy of the lift.

Ethan stared after her, a small smile hovering on his lips. It seemed little Miss Adams might prove more of a challenge than he'd thought. There was something about her . . . Yes, she would suit him very nicely once he'd disabused her of a few liberated notions. He picked up a ruler, slapped it absently on his thigh, then laid it down again. Fortunately she was by no means a fool, and she wouldn't throw away the kind of money he was offering over an issue as trivial as making his coffee. He would soon have that nonsense knocked out of her. Not literally, of course. He had no respect for men who used their physical superiority in order to get what they wanted. Apart from which, there were more subtle methods of dealing with dissident staff.

He closed the door behind Holly and went to stare out of the window. It was dark, and rain glistened in the beam of the lamplight far below. As he gazed down, looking at nothing in particular, he was assaulted by a sudden sense of *déjà vu*. The street had looked just that way on the day he'd found out about Alice . . . His jaw hardened and he pressed his hands down on the sill.

Alice . . . No, dammit, that little gold-digger wasn't going to get to him now — or ever again. He'd wasted too many hours of his youth on that worthless creature.

Frowning, he ran a hand round the back of his neck, and gradually the tension in his body began to ease. Thank God he had found plain little Holly Adams, with the sweet smile and the enormous eyes, who was as different from Alice as diamonds were different from coal. With Holly there was no danger of a repeat of that long-ago folly. He wasn't a boy any longer — and his new assistant wasn't his type. As she had certainly made it clear he wasn't hers.

No tea, coffee, dry-cleaning or gifts indeed! His frown vanished and he grinned into the gathering shadows.

Then he returned to his desk, reached for a pen, and after a moment's contemplation began to write.

Miss Adams was in for a surprise.

★　★　★

Holly thought about wearing her best plum-coloured suit for her first day on the job, but in the end she decided against it. She might as well start as she meant to go on, by making no particular concessions to Mr Yorke's already inflated ego. Her sensible brown would do him very well.

He wasn't in his office when she

knocked, so she sat down at the desk she had dubbed the dragon's lair — before she became the dragon herself.

It was equipped with all the standard appendages of office life: files, pencils, pens, telephone and an assortment of notebooks. A computer terminal had been added since yesterday as well. Holly sighed. It wasn't home yet, but she supposed she would learn to get used to it.

She stood up and headed automatically for the coffee-maker she had noted in an alcove off Mr Yorke's office. She needed a cup to kick-start her day, and it wasn't until the mellow brown liquid was running promisingly into a carafe that she remembered she hadn't meant to make coffee. She was staring doubtfully down at the delectable stream, wondering what she ought to do about it, when a voice behind her said, 'Excellent, Miss Adams. I see you've come to your senses. Bring me a cup when it's ready, will you? And I'd like you to type up these letters.'

Holly turned around slowly and took the Dictaphone tape out of his hand. 'It was an accident,' she explained.

'What was?'

'The coffee. I made it without thinking.'

'Splendid. Then perhaps you could get on with those letters without thinking. You seem to do remarkably well when you put your thought processes on hold. Keep it up.' He sauntered over to his desk and sat down.

Holly glared at the right side of his face. His long eyelashes swept over his cheekbone, and he was staring down at several pages of scribble on a pad. He appeared to be oblivious to her presence. The coffee-machine clicked off, and she poured a cup for herself and started to cross the white carpet to the door.

'Miss Adams, you forgot my coffee.' The firm voice halted her in her tracks.

'It's not in my job description,' said Holly, not quite believing that she, Holly Adams, was actually refusing to oblige him. No one else in the office would believe it either. Whenever anyone wanted anything done, they always came to Holly, because they knew she could never bring herself to refuse help wherever it was needed. But Mr Yorke had a very different effect on her good nature. Around him she seemed to shift into reverse.

'Miss Adams.' He sounded bored. 'Would you care to come over here? I'd like you to look at something.'

Holly wouldn't care, but she put the cup down and went anyway, because he was pointing at a printed page displayed on the corner of his desk.

'Read it,' he said, and went on perusing his scribble.

Holly read it. It was a revised version of the job description for presidential assistant. The last paragraph read,

Make and serve tea and coffee as the need arises. Purchase and/or deliver supplies, personal or otherwise, as required by the president.

'You see,' he said blandly when she had finished reading. 'It's all perfectly legal.'

'You've had it changed,' she accused him.

'Mmm.' He noted something on his pad. 'So I have.'

'But you've no right — '

'I have every right. I hired you to do a job for me, Miss Adams. That's part of it. You'll regret it if you expect me to make the coffee.'

'Is that a threat?'

'You might say so. I make terrible coffee.'

Holly, who had been glaring at the job description, looked up quickly, just in time to catch a hint of a smile on his face before he wiped it ruthlessly away.

'Is that the truth?' she asked, folding a corner of the paper.

'Try me and find out.'

She shook her head. 'No. It's all right, I believe you.'

'Good.' He went on writing, and reluctantly Holly returned to the coffee-maker to pour a second cup.

He was right. It *was* up to him to decide what her job would involve. If she didn't like it she could always quit. But at the thought of leaving Smart and Yorke's her heart did a funny little flop — so after delivering his coffee she turned her back on him and hurried out to her desk.

Half an hour later she returned to his office, put the completed letters in front of him, and said woodenly, 'I hope you don't mind, Mr Yorke, but I've made some changes.'

'I expected you to,' he replied without looking up.

'You did?' Holly blinked.

'Mmm. Spelling has never been my strong point.' He pulled the letters towards him and after a moment smiled drily. 'I see my composition doesn't impress you either.'

'Well, I just thought — '

'Don't apologise. You've done very well. See if you can do as well with these figures.'

As Holly took the work from him their fingers touched. She pulled them away quickly, wondering if he'd done it on purpose to test her reaction. But his head was already bent over his desk again, and he seemed totally absorbed by a computer print-out. She took a decp breath and departed for her lair, wondering if she had just witnessed the lion turning into the lamb, or the wolf donning his sheep's clothing. In any case, Mr Yorke was no lamb. He was a real live male chauvinist of the arrogant kind. But if he was handled right she was sure she'd be able to manage him.

A month later she wasn't sure who was managing whom.

They got along surprisingly well, but when Holly stopped to think about it it occurred to her that whatever Mr Yorke wanted he got.

She had told him she wouldn't make coffee, but she was making it. He had asked her to pick up his shirts and she had picked them up because he had stained the one he was wearing with felt pen just half an hour before an important meeting. It had seemed unkind to refuse to fetch them when he was so busy. Then he had forgotten to buy a gift for his sister's birthday, and he had looked so stricken that Holly had offered to do it for him before she remembered that she had distinctly heard him tell Ellen Yorke that she didn't deserve a damn thing for her birthday.

On the other hand, although he was inclined to hand her a job to do and expect it yesterday, his ego was not so overwhelming that he found it necessary to object when she made cosmetic changes to his work. He even seemed to appreciate her efforts. In fact Holly came to the conclusion that, as far as Mr Yorke was concerned, he had his assistant exactly where he wanted her. He was, as she had known he would be, a hard taskmaster, in that he never allowed her a single unoccupied moment. But he paid her to work hard, and she couldn't complain that he was unfair.

So why, she wondered, did she often feel a totally unwarranted urge to punch his rather broad nose? In the end she decided it was just her own instinctive reaction to good-looking, self-assured men. It was, Tom, the handsomest boy at her school, who had once dubbed her 'Butterball Holly'. For a long time the name had stuck, even though she'd lost some weight since those agonising puppy-fat days. Another time, a Greek god in the post-room had referred to her as Holly the Hopeless — and she knew she wasn't hopeless. She was a damned good employee who got the job done. And of course there had been Andy . . .

No, she wasn't partial to handsome hunks.

At close to four o'clock on the last day of Holly's trial period, she heard her boss slam down the phone more forcefully than usual and let out a stream of the kind of language that made her want to cover her ears. She gasped. It wasn't like Mr Yorke to lose his temper. She wondered if whatever had angered him was about to erupt over her.

It was.

'Adams,' he said, striding out of his office and coming to lean over her desk, 'why didn't I get that message from Diane Darcy?'

'Message?' said Holly blankly.

'That's what I said. The one letting me know she wouldn't be able to make it to the play tonight.'

'I don't know why you didn't get it.' Holly gave him a frosty smile. 'I put it on your desk. I also called it to your attention. You grunted. I expect you accidentally threw it out.'

'Don't make excuses, Adams, and don't try to cover your mistakes. Diane says she phoned yesterday at lunchtime. I bought the tickets yesterday evening.' He pressed a fist into her blotter and glared down at her.

'She did phone, and I gave you the message,' said Holly calmly. 'And I don't appreciate being called a liar, Mr Yorke. Nor do I appreciate being called Adams. I am either Holly or *Ms* Adams to you.'

For a moment she thought he was going to explode. His brown eyes blazed, and his dark complexion turned several shades darker. When he reached over to take her arm, she was reminded of the look on her father's face when her immediate future was about to become unpredictable. She started as his fingers curved around her elbow and a surprising sizzle of something that was more excitement than fear made her squirm and try to pull away.

'Oh, for heaven's sake.' He let her go abruptly. 'Stop looking at me as if you think I'm about to beat you.'

'I thought you might be,' she admitted, releasing her breath.

'Adams.' He leaned over her, but this time he didn't touch her. 'Adams, you are a fool. Smart and Yorke is not a nineteenth-century sweat-shop. You have, on occasions, got my goat, but on the whole I'm quite satisfied with your work. And even if I weren't, I doubt if you could reduce me to violence.'

'No, of course not,' said Holly, confused by a sudden awareness that her boss in this ominous mood was having a very curious effect on her pulse-rate. All the same, some small streak of stubbornness made her mutter, 'But my name still isn't Adams.'

'Hmm.' He grabbed her elbow again, but seemed not to notice it. 'All right, *Holly*, what the devil did you do with my message?'

'I told you. I put it on your desk. And if you don't choose to believe me . . . ' Because the touch of his firm fingers was too disturbing, she shrugged him off and stood up.

'Yes? If I don't choose to believe you?' He raised a questioning and coolly provoking eyebrow.

Holly swallowed. He didn't look angry any more; he looked . . . speculative. As if he was wondering how indignant he could make her. Well, maybe *he* found the situation entertaining, but she was damned if she would let him call her a liar.

'I'll have no choice but to leave,' she finished bravely, turning away so he wouldn't see the brightness in her eyes.

To her consternation, he responded by coming round the desk, cupping her cheeks, and twisting her head firmly to face him. As soon as he was sure he had her attention, he let her go. 'Don't be an idiot,' he said crisply. 'I was in a bad temper. I apologise if I hurt your feelings.'

'Do you always go around calling people liars when you're in a bad temper?' demanded Holly, who found she was breathing a little faster than usual.

'Not people, no. Just you. Don't ask me why.'

Holly didn't need to ask him why. It was the way his sort of man had always treated her — either as a near-invisible doormat or as a scapegoat. She'd long since ceased to expect anything better from the more glamorous members of the opposite sex, and she wondered why it mattered so much now.

Suddenly it was important for him not to guess that he'd hurt her.

'Don't worry about it,' she said with an assumption of indifference — and a strong notion that he wasn't worrying at all. 'I don't know what happened to your message, but I'm sure it's very annoying to be saddled with tickets you can't use.'

'Yes.' He rubbed a pensive hand over his jaw and eyed her shrewdly. 'Almost as annoying as being called a liar. But I believe I have a solution to both our problems.'

'What's that?' Holly refused to look at him.

'You come to the play with me instead.'

Holly's head jerked upwards, but she still kept her eyes averted. 'Instead of what?' she asked, in what she hoped was an uninterested voice. She knew perfectly well that the answer was, Instead of Diane.

'Instead of sitting at home brooding over the disgraceful behaviour of your boss.'

'I never brood,' said Holly. She thought about telling him she wouldn't be sitting at home either, but it wasn't true, and she had just assured him she wasn't a liar.

'Don't you? In that case you won't object to seeing Penelope Kelly's new comedy. Or are you afraid it may make you laugh?'

Oh, so now she lacked a sense of humour, did she? 'Of course not,' she snapped. 'Penelope Kelly is one of my favourite comediennes. But — '

'But your nose is out of joint and you don't want to go anywhere with me. Especially if it might actually oblige me. Is that it?'

Holly slanted a quick glance at his face. His expression was totally dead-pan, yet she had the impression that he was secretly amused. His brown eyes gleamed, and suddenly she found herself wanting to laugh with him as she hadn't laughed since she started this job. And now that she thought about it, it was ages since she'd been to a play. Mr Yorke wouldn't be that difficult to get along with for one evening, and it would be a pity to let his tickets go to waste.

'Not at all. I'll be happy to oblige you,' she said, suppressing a smile and folding her hands demurely in front of her. 'What time would you like me to meet you?'

'Ah. That's better. I haven't much patience with sulks.' He nodded approvingly and glanced at his watch. 'How about I drive you home now? Then you can change and we'll have an early dinner before the play.'

'Dinner?' squeaked Holly. She hadn't counted on that.

'Of course. Didn't you expect me to feed you?'

'I hadn't thought about it,' Holly

admitted. 'All right. It does seem the most sensible arrangement. I'll just go and tidy my desk.'

She dodged round him and began to shuffle papers into piles. Then a feeling of being watched made her pause and glance over her shoulder.

Mr Yorke was standing in the doorway of his office with a very odd look on his face. An almost dumbfounded look — as if he couldn't believe he had actually asked his quiet little assistant to go out with him. Not that he had asked her in the usual sense. He'd just decided she would do to fill a troublesome gap in his social agenda.

Holly turned away. She didn't feel like laughing any longer. Diane Darcy, after all, was a blonde and scintillating model. Holly Adams was an unobtrusive toiler at a desk — not his usual line in ladies, and probably he already regretted his impulsive invitation.

Too bad for him. Holly flipped a paper-clip into a tray and tossed her hair back, because she intended to make the best of this evening. For once in her life Holly Adams was going to be seen in public escorted by one of London's most eligible men. And if he proved as difficult in a social setting as he frequently was in the office — well, she was more than capable of giving back as good as she got.

Ten minutes later she was seated in Ethan Yorke's sleek white Maserati as he manoeuvred it out on to the street. She stretched her legs and leaned back against the soft leather upholstery. This was a style with which she could very easily become quite comfortable, she decided, especially as Mr Yorke chose not to interrupt her enjoyment of the drive by making polite — or in his case, no doubt, irritating — conversation. Instead he drove quickly and efficiently through rush-hour traffic and drew up in front of her brother's house with just the barest pressure on the brakes.

'Did you drive a racing car in another life?' asked Holly, unwilling to admit she was impressed.

He grinned. 'I don't think so. But I do in this one.'

Oh. Yes, so he did. She remembered now. The office had been buzzing about a year ago, when he'd won some prestigious race she'd forgotten the name of. She hadn't cared at the time.

'Yes, of course,' she said quickly, wishing she'd remembered. 'Er — would you like to come in while I change?' Suddenly she felt awkward. Noel and Barbara were bound to get the wrong idea and assume she had a date with her boss. And Mr Yorke would probably raise those extraordinary eyebrows of his and make some predictably cutting remark when he encountered the casual clutter of the house. 'Maybe you should wait in the car,' she amended quickly.

'And maybe I shouldn't.' He took her arm. 'Hurry up, Adams, I don't like eating on the run.'

'My name is Holly,' she replied, allowing him to lead her up the crazy-paving path with the weeds growing up between the cracks.

'Right. And mine's Ethan.'

Holly stopped and gazed up at him with her mouth hanging open. When she saw he was looking at her with that quizzical little gleam she was becoming used to, she gulped and mumbled stupidly, 'I know it is — Mr Yorke.'

'You don't listen, do you? Not Mr Yorke. Ethan.'

'But I can't call you that.'

'Why not? Is there something wrong with Ethan?'

'But — you're my boss.'

'I know, and I don't intend for you to forget it. However, since this is a social occasion, I think a little informality can be permitted. In fact, I'd prefer it.'

'I wouldn't,' said Holly, who couldn't see herself calling this controlled and authoritative powerhouse by his first name.'

'Just do as you're told,' he said wearily, taking her arm again and marching her up the path to the front door. 'I don't propose to spend the rest of the evening entertaining a young lady who insists on reminding me of the office.'

'You don't have to entertain me,' said Holly stiffly.

'I'll remember that.' He watched interestedly as she groped in her bag for her key and opened the door. 'You, on the other had, are expected to entertain me.'

'Oh, you want me to sing for my supper, do you?' jeered Holly as she led him into the kitchen. She had intended to install him in the sitting room, but if he was so determined to be informal, Chris and the cats and the kitchen would serve him right. Except that, unaccountably, Chris and the cats were not there.

'That would be nice,' he agreed blandly, settling himself at the table and stretching his legs. 'How about 'Greensleeves?''

''Greensleeves' always makes me sad,' said Holly without thinking. Then she added venomously, 'And if I sang it, it would make *you* even sadder.'

His lips quirked. 'Ah. Singing is not among your accomplishments, then, I gather. Never mind, I'll settle for conversation and suitable deference to my wishes. In other words, Holly, you will damn well call me Ethan.'

He was smiling now, but it was a totally implacable smile, and Holly had no doubt that he meant it.

'Oh, very well,' she said. 'If it makes you happy.'

'That's much better. I like my women to make me happy.'

'But I'm not your woman,' she pointed out, wondering why that irrefutable truth made her feel unexpectedly flat. 'Diane is.'

'Right. So you're filling in for her.'

Holly was already on her way to the door, but she turned around quickly, not sure whether he was teasing or serious. He was grinning broadly, and she turned away again. How could she have been so foolish as to believe, even

59

for a moment, that a man like Ethan would ever regard her as a substitute for the gorgeous Diane? Of course he had her neatly labelled 'assistant' not 'woman'. His type were all like that.

She stamped upstairs to her room and went to put on her only good dress.

Sighing, she studied her reflection in the mirror. The dress was made of dark green wool, severely cut so as not to emphasise her figure, with a V neck and long straight sleeves. She looked like a well-fed owl, she decided glumly. Barbara had told her several times that she ought to get more flattering glasses, but Holly had never seen the sense. The ones she had were a practical aid to eyesight, which was all she cared about.

Mr Yorke — Ethan — would just have to take her as she was.

When she reached the kitchen she saw at once that the cats had reappeared. Both of them were sitting on the table in front of Ethan, fixing him with their unblinking yellow eyes. He was returning the look with one that she could only call dubious.

'I'm sorry. Don't you like cats?' she asked.

'Cats are fine in their place. Which isn't on the table.'

Holly was inclined to agree with him, but they were Noel's and Barbara's cats, and immediately she found herself rising to her feline friends' defence. 'It's their house too,' she informed him.

'And not mine? True. A mercy for which I assure you I'm suitably thankful.'

'Annie Holly, Annie Holly!' A piping child's voice, following by the piping child, burst into the room before Holly could come up with a retort. There was a second's pause and then the voice said accusingly, 'Annie Holly, you're going out.'

'Yes,' agreed Holly. 'Chris, this is Mr Yorke.'

To her surprise, Ethan held out his hand to the small blond boy and said gravely, 'If you don't mind, I *would* like to take your aunty Holly out. Do you think you could lend her to me for a short while?'

'How long is a while?' asked Chris. 'Will she be back in the morning?'

Holly heard Barbara, who had just come into the hallway, mutter, 'Let's hope not.'

'Yes, of course I will, Chris,' she said hastily. 'And a while is only a few hours.'

'I'll take good care of her,' Ethan assured the sceptical child.

'Well, OK. I s'pose we can share her.' Chris frowned. 'Mr Yolk?'

'Mmm?'

'Mr Yolk, don't you think that, besides my mummy, my annie Holly is the most beautiful lady in the whole world?'

Holly's face heated up as if someone had put a match to it, and she hurried out into the hall so she wouldn't have to hear Ethan's answer.

But even though she put both hands over her ears his deep voice followed her.

'Of course I do, Chris. She finds things for me that I've lost, makes my coffee, corrects my spelling — and just about everything else — and she takes my messages and remembers all my appointments. I don't know how I'd manage without her.'

'Oh,' said Chris. 'You mean she's just like a mummy.'

Ethan's laugh rang out, loud and unrestrained. 'Yes,' he agreed. 'I guess you could put it that way.'

3

'They'll fall out if you grind them much harder,' observed Ethan, as he swung the car neatly into what appeared to be the last parking space left in London.

'What will?' asked Holly coldly.

'Your teeth.'

She pressed her lips together and refused to answer.

'Why do I get the feeling that you'd very much like to sink them into me?' he asked, almost as if he was talking to himself.

'I've no idea,' said Holly, who had no intention of telling him that she resented being classified as somebody's mother. Especially his. He wouldn't understand. For that matter, she didn't really understand herself. All she knew was that when she had overhead his amused response to her nephew's innocent remark she had felt a burning desire to steam back into the kitchen and shout at him that she wasn't anybody's mother and never would be — because in order to be a mother she would first of all need to find a man. Preferably a husband. And as she had no interest in acquiring one of those overrated disturbers of single bliss, she certainly didn't intend to be a mother.

Barbara, coming into the hall, had seen the look on her face and forcibly held her back, and a moment later Ethan had strolled into the hall, taken her arm, and steered her back out to the car — where she had sat glaring malevolently at oblivious passers-by and, according to Ethan, grinding her teeth.

'Come on,' he said, moving round to open her door. 'I won't let you bite me, but you can work off some of that bad temper on a steak.'

'I don't like steak,' said Holly, rejecting the hand he extended to help her out.

'Fine. You can work it off on a

plateful of pasta for all I care, but you're not taking it out on me.' He grabbed her arm, slammed the door behind her, and started to march her across the busy street. As the wind whipped at her coat, his thigh pressed briefly against her hip, and she was startled at how right it felt there: firm, lending confidence — and something else that was totally unfamiliar. She moistened her lips. Then she saw that they were heading for one of the smartest restaurants in Soho, and confidence became a thing of the past. In her plain green dress she would look like a weed among the orchids.

In fact it wasn't that bad. She only looked like a cucumber amid the buttered asparagus. And Ethan didn't seem to notice.

'OK,' he said, when they were seated in an alcove at a table laid with spotless linen, gleaming silverware and a centre-piece of fresh hothouse flowers, 'let's have it. What have I done to upset you?'

Holly waited until they had given

their orders to an attentive waiter and then said frigidly, 'Nothing.'

'Rot. You've been sulking ever since we left your brother's house.'

'I don't sulk.'

'Oh? You also told me you don't brood. The fact is, you've been doing one or the other for the past forty-five minutes. I've had about enough of it, my dear.'

Holly sighed and stared down at the table. Ethan was right. She *had* been brooding, which was something she rarely did. And it wasn't his fault. How could he know that his remark would hurt her? For that matter, why *was* she hurt? He'd been paying her a compliment in his way.

'I'm sorry,' she said, looking up to meet an unamused chestnut-brown gaze.

Ethan studied her for a few minutes, his gaze keen and assessing, and as she watched him she saw the habitual hardness of his features begin to soften.

'What is it, Holly?' he asked. 'You're

not usually given to playing the prima donna. That was one of the reasons I took you on in the first place.'

She wanted to repeat that it was nothing, but somehow, with those formidable brown eyes demanding a prompt and reasonable answer, she found herself admitting the truth.

'I didn't like you agreeing with Chris — about me being some sort of secretarial mother.'

He frowned. 'Why ever not? I didn't mean it literally.'

'I know.' She picked up a fork and put it down again. 'I suppose . . . maybe it's just that I'm not — won't ever be — anyone's mother.'

'What?' To her surprise, he reached across the table to take her hand. 'Holly, how can you possibly know that?'

Holly stared at him. His eyes were warm now, so was the feel of his hand, and his lips were firm and unconsciously seductive. For no reason, she felt a lump form in her throat. 'Because

I'll never have a husband,' she said.

'Why do you say that?' His forehead creased. 'You must have boyfriends.'

She shook her head. 'The closest I ever came to a boyfriend was Andy next door. We were childhood playmates and we used to talk about getting married when we grew up. I thought he meant it. I adored him. And then we did grow up, and he fell in love with the greengrocer's beautiful daughter. After that I made up my mind I wouldn't even think about marriage.'

Holly took off her glasses and dashed a hand over her eyes as she tried desperately to blot out the memory of Andy's betrayal. He'd been so handsome and funny, they were such good friends, and she'd been sure he'd ask her to the sixth-form dance. But when she'd mentioned it to him, full of trust and innocent adoration, he'd looked surprised, and said he was going with Adele. It hadn't even occurred to him that Holly might expect to be invited. Later, she had seen him kissing the greengrocer's daughter, and that evening, her face splotched with big, bruising tears, she had looked in the mirror and seen what she supposed Andy must have seen — not the lovely Adele, but an owl-eyed child with shiny cheeks and mouse-coloured hair. No wonder he hadn't thought of taking her to the dance. Holly remembered that in the end she had dried her tears, squared her shoulders, and vowed to forget about men, and concentrate on things she was good at. She didn't need a man to give her life meaning.

Since then, she had consciously avoided situations that might lead to her being hurt again. Andy had eventually married Adele, and shortly after the school year ended Noel and Holly had left the Hertfordshire town where they'd grown up, to work in London.

Strange, she hadn't cried about Andy, or thought about him much, in years. Until today . . .

She started, and came back to the

present. Ethan was watching her closely — too closely. 'I'm sorry,' she muttered. 'I didn't mean to bore you with the story of my life.'

She hadn't meant to, either. Although at the time she'd been sure she'd die of grief, she really was over Andy. So why had she lost control now — in front of her boss?

'You're not boring me,' he said. 'Holly, you're only twenty-three. There's still time.'

He smiled, a sympathetic, mildly exasperated smile, as if she were a little girl who had fallen and scraped her knee. But she wasn't a child.

'No, there *isn't* time,' she said, the words tumbling out without thought. 'I'm just not the type men propose to. And anyway, I'm quite happy with my career.'

Lord, why had she said that? It made her sound self-pitying. And she *didn't* want to be proposed to. She *had* been quite happy with her career until tonight. She was good at her job and had risen very quickly within the firm. Ever since Andy, she had been quite sure that would be enough.

'I'm glad to hear it,' Ethan was saying, not looking as if he believed her. 'But if marriage really is what you want, I've no doubt the right man will come along.'

He did sound bored now — patronising as well — as if she were indeed a fretful child. Without even knowing it was going to happen, Holly exploded. 'Oh, sure. I suppose next you're going to tell me you'd marry me yourself if you weren't already engaged to Diane.'

His eyebrows shot up and Holly clapped a hand across her mouth. She was just starting to rise, intending to make a bolt for the ladies' room, when the soup arrived.

'Sit down,' said Ethan curtly. 'There's no need to make an exhibition of yourself. Or of me.'

Holly sat, and without a word he poured her a glass of wine.

'Drink,' he said.

Holly drank, and as the dry white liquid slid down her throat she felt the colour rise up her neck and suffuse her face.

'I'm sorry,' she said, managing to keep her voice steady. 'Of course I didn't mean that.'

'Of course not.' He lifted his glass. 'Now, then, let's put a stop to this nonsense once and for all.'

She nodded.

'In the first place, and just so there's no misunderstanding, I am not engaged to Diane. She's someone I take out occasionally. That's all. In the second place, I wouldn't ask you to marry me if you were Helen of Troy. I don't believe in office romances. In the third place, you have to stop being so damn self-deprecating. You're no raving beauty, thank heavens, but you're competent and intelligent and you have nice legs — and a remarkably attractive smile.'

Holly tried to suppress a ridiculous glow of pleasure. 'You don't approve of legs,' she pointed out.

Ethan bit the corner of his lip, and she wondered if he was trying not to laugh.

'What I approve or disapprove of is not the issue,' he replied equably. 'I have no particular aversion to legs. As a matter of fact I rather enjoy them. I just don't like them doing high kicks around my office. It's too distracting. What *is* the point is your absurd lack of confidence in yourself. I — '

'I don't lack confidence.' Holly tried to smile brightly, but had a horrible feeling that her efforts only made her look like a moon-faced coquette on the make. She pushed at her hair, and hastily picked up her spoon, not liking what she recognised as a dawning glint of suspicion in Ethan's eye.

'This isn't some devious plot to get me to the altar, I hope?' he said softly.

Holly laced her fingers beneath the table. She had known the smile was unfortunate, but who did this man think he was? Adonis? Every woman's ideal heart-throb? If so, he needed taking down a peg. Several pegs.

'I'm not that desperate,' she retorted, raising her eyebrows and trying to look as though she were indeed Helen of Troy rejecting an objectionable suitor.

'Thank you.' His eyebrows rose too. 'As long as we understand each other. When I mentioned your many excellent qualities, did I remember to point out that one of them is not flattering the ego of your boss?'

Holly watched the waiter remove her bowl and managed to answer calmly, 'I'm glad you appreciate that. You should understand, Mr Yorke, that being accused of plotting matrimony is quite a new experience for me. I'm beginning to think this evening was a mistake.'

'Only if we allow it to be. I admit I had no right to suggest you were after my assets, but I'm afraid that sort of thing is *not* a new experience for me.' He patted her hand in a way that she supposed was meant to disarm her.

'Come on, eat up and try to be merry. We'll just have to make the best of each other.'

Holly nodded, and produced a frozen little smile. She supposed he was right. After this rocky start, surely the rest of the night could only get better.

For a while it did. They conversed amiably throughout the remainder of the meal, and Holly discovered that Ethan could be an amusing and entertaining companion when it happened to suit him.

The play, as expected, was light and funny, and soon Holly forgot the company she was in and gave way to uninhibited laughter. Once or twice she caught Ethan's eyes on her and they laughed together. By the time it was over she had begun to think her boss might actually be human, which was about the best she could expect of any attractive man. At least tonight he was aware that she existed as more than a convenient factotum. It made a pleasant change.

Afterwards he suggested a drink at a nightclub, but Holly decided not to push her luck. Things were going amicably between them and it seemed wisest to bring the evening to a close.

'No, thank you. It's getting late,' she told him sedately.

'And you want to be fresh and alert to do my bidding in the morning, is that it? How very gratifying.'

'No, I want to be fresh and alert to keep you in your place in the morning,' she replied deflatingly. He was teasing her, of course, but there was no reason to let him get away with it, even if he was the president of a multinational empire.

But Ethan only chuckled. He wasn't an easy man to deflate.

They were in the theatre lobby, about to pass into the street, when Holly heard him swear, softly and very explicitly.

She looked up, startled, and saw that he was staring across the lobby at a radiant blonde on the arm of a tall dark man.

Alice Adonidas. Holly knew her at once. Her picture was in the papers all the time. She was married to Theodore Adonidas, the shipping magnate. Holly turned to look at Alice's escort. Yes, that was her husband, reputed to be one of the richest men in the world. Sensing the instant tension in the man beside her, she looked up at him and saw that the chandelier over their heads had cast a glittering cold light across his face. It was mask-like, utterly without warmth, as if he had been turned into marble.

Suddenly Alice Adonidas seemed to sense that she was being watched. She started, and looked round until her eyes connected with Ethan's. Immediately her gaze shifted sideways to settle with overplayed surprise on Holly's short and unimpressive figure. Her eyebrows lifted, and she gave Ethan a faintly derisive smile before taking her husband's arm and leaving the theatre without a word.

'Why are you looking at me as if you think I'm about to jump off a bridge?'

asked Ethan harshly, as he led Holly across the lobby and out into the drizzle that had followed the wind. 'It's not going to happen, you know. I haven't time for headline-grabbing histrionics.'

'You know Alice Adonidas, don't you?' said Holly, ignoring the cold brutality of his words.

'I used to.'

'And she hurt you.' So certain was Holly of this that she spoke without even thinking.

'Did she?' he jeered. 'Then I hope you won't be too disappointed if I decline to tell you all the gory details.'

He made it sound as though she were a nosy little busybody, instead of a friend who wanted to help. And the look of disdain Alice had thrown at her had hurt too. It was as if she was sneering at Ethan because he hadn't found a more distinguished date.

'No, I won't be disappointed,' she said dully.

Ethan threw her a look that was part exasperation and part contrition and hurried her across the street to his car.

As they sped through the streets, damp with rain in the cool midnight air, Holly studied him out of the corner of her eye. His mouth was hard, unsmiling, but she couldn't detect a hint of real emotion in the bleak gaze fixed on the road. Either he was more adept at hiding his feelings than she'd realised, or Alice Adonidas was a ghost who had brought back unpleasant memories, but no longer had a hold on his heart.

Holly stared at his unreadable profile and wondered if that heart had ever been capable of a lasting attachment. He was thirty-two and unmarried, rumour had it that he'd had a succession of beautiful girlfriends, and it was likely that permanent commitment had never been high on his agenda. Which, from her point of view, was just as well. She had already been manipulated into shopping for his father and sister on several occasions. She could imagine what kind of trouble a wife could be.

'Holly . . . '

'Ethan . . . '

Both of them spoke at once and then paused, waiting for the other to continue. Their eyes met briefly, and in that moment of distraction a dark shape darted into the road. A black cat, in too much of hurry to wait until they passed, narrowly avoided the front wheels. Then another shape, a young girl this time, shot out in frantic pursuit.

'Ethan!' screamed Holly. 'She's going to . . . '

But Ethan had seen the girl too. He flicked the steering-wheel, swerved to the right, and in a brilliantly skilful manoeuvre, ended up back in the left lane.

Holly was about to heave a sigh of relief when Ethan said, 'Hell,' and his arm slammed across her chest, pinning her back against the seat.

Behind them, brakes squealed on the wet paving. Holly threw a horrified glance at the side-mirror and saw the lights of a large vehicle swerve crazily and head straight towards them.

Tyres screeched, her head snapped back, and her knees slammed up against the dashboard.

When she came to, she was in a hospital bed, and the morning sun was streaming through the window.

★ ★ ★

'Bye, Holly. Don't worry, the doctor says you'll be fine in a couple of months. As long as you stay clear of cars and my mother's pumpernickel soup.'

Holly nodded sleepily and tried to smile. 'I will. Thanks, Barbara.' She closed her eyes, and at once her mind went back to the moment when she had regained consciousness and been told by someone — she couldn't remember who — that she had broken her ankle but had managed not to break her neck — which still felt uncommonly stiff.

Now her leg was encased in a cast, and she was in a ward whose most audible occupant was an elderly lady with her arm in a cast who kept insisting, shrilly, that someone had stolen her last cigarette.

'What the devil are you doing in here?'

Holly jumped as an authoritative voice snapped across the room and a sharp pain ran up her leg.

'What do you think I'm doing?' she asked, as her last foggy hopes of sleep dropped away, and Ethan marched up to the bed looking as if he'd just conquered a boardroom. 'Sunbathing on the Riviera?'

'Don't be cheeky. It doesn't suit you.'

'Neither does a broken ankle.'

'Hmm. I get the distinct impression you're going to live for a long time.' He pushed a hand through his hair and scowled down at her. 'I'm sorry about the ankle.'

'It wasn't your fault.'

He shrugged. 'Just the same, it was

hardly the way I planned for the evening to end.'

'Oh? What did you have planned?' she asked puzzled. 'I thought we were on our way home.'

His scowl deepened. 'Nothing compromising, if that's what you mean.'

'Of course it isn't.' Holly buried her face in the pillow to hide a blush. 'And you didn't have to tell me that, Ethan. I don't do compromising.'

'I suspected as much,' he said drily. 'Now kindly answer my question. What are you doing in this ward when I specifically ordered a private room?'

'It seems your orders were specifically ignored.' Holly resented the implication that she had somehow subverted his authority. Besides, her ankle was hurting and she was in no mood to cope with Ethan's ego.

'Not for long they won't be,' he said tersely. 'You're going to have the best care available.

As Holly's mouth fell open, he turned his back and strode out into the corridor. She could hear his feet slamming against the hard hospital floor.

The old woman who wanted her cigarettes started thumping her bedside table. When that brought no results, she pushed back the bedclothes and began to sidle across the ward.

When Holly closed her eyes, she felt bony hands fumbling beneath her pillow. She grunted and turned over, and the old woman tiptoed away.

By the time Ethan reappeared some twenty minutes later, Holly had almost dropped off to sleep.

Ethan didn't tiptoe, and at once she was jolted wide awake.

'It's settled,' he said. 'They'll be moving you this afternoon.

'What if I don't want to be moved?' asked Holly, who wanted very much to get away from the tiresome elderly smoker, but didn't appreciate the decision being taken out of her hands.

'Don't you?' asked Ethan, looking thunderstruck.

'Don't I what?'

'Don't you want me to take you by the scruff of the neck and shake you?' he groaned.

'Not particularly. My neck's not in very good shape.'

'Then for heaven's sake tell me whether you'd like to be moved to a private room or not.' His fist closed around the rail beside the bed.

Holly considered saying not but thought better of it. 'I can't afford it,' she said in the end.

'I don't expect you to afford it. Since the company got you into this predicament, the company's paying.'

'I thought *you* got me into this predicament,' said Holly, unfairly.

He straightened his shoulders and she guessed he was trying not to lose his temper. 'It's the same thing. Now do you want to be moved or don't you?'

The old lady shouted, 'Nurse! I insist that you return my cigarettes. If you don't I'm going to be sick.'

'Yes, please,' said Holly hastily.

'Thank you. I didn't mean to be — '

'Obstructive, contrary and a damned nuisance?' suggested Ethan. 'Good. I much prefer you capable, efficient and obliging.'

'As in slavish?' She didn't bother to dilute the acid.

'As in helpful and pleasant to be around.

'Did you say kick around?' Holly couldn't seem to stop twisting everything he said. She knew it annoyed him and she wanted to annoy him without in the least understanding why.

He leaned over and seemed about to reach for her shoulders. Then he took a deep breath, flexed his fingers, and straightened slowly. 'We'll leave the kicking until you've recovered,' he said flatly. 'You can expect it. Meanwhile, as I meant to tell you last night, you can consider yourself my permanent assistant. I assume you would like the job?'

Holly wished she could tell him that she wouldn't like it in the least. But she knew she had to accept. The pay was phenomenal, and Noel and Barbara needed all the financial help they could get. Besides, she liked working for Ethan, in spite of his carelessly chauvinistic ways. He was a man who knew his mind and got things done. In the last year of his father's presidency it had been difficult to get any decisions made. Now the complaint she heard most often was that the president expected his decisions to be implemented almost before he had made them.

'Thank you,' she said. 'You can consider your appointment permanent as well.'

For a moment, as he glared round the room as if he were searching for something to throw, she wondered if perhaps she'd gone too far. It was all very well reminding him that she hadn't been the only one on probation, but missiles launched in a hospital ward were not likely to go down well with the National Health.

However, when he turned back to

face her, she was astounded to see that his brown eyes were gleaming with mirth. 'First blood to you,' he said gravely. 'All right, Ms Adams, since even *I* can't expect you to tramp round my office on one leg, whom do you suggest I hire to replace you? Temporarily, of course.'

'Oh,' said Holly.

'That, my dear, is not an answer.'

'No. I suppose Hilda Thomas in Marketing could do it.'

'The brunette with the legs? No, thanks, I'm much too used to yours. I find them both pleasing and familiar.'

Holly lowered her eyelashes. He was teasing her, of course, but she didn't know how to respond. That sort of mildly suggestive compliment had never come her way. And she was amazed to find that his words sent a quick jolt of pleasure up her spine.

'Solange Peters, then,' she said quickly, deciding to ignore his banter. 'She's good at figures. Or Michael Molton in Sales.'

'Solange Peters may be good at figures, but I doubt if I'd function well with an assistant who ducks under her desk to search for non-existent paper-clips the moment she sees me approach. And Michael is much too useful where he is.'

'Then you'd better ask Miss Lovejoy to phone an employment agency,' said Holly. This conversation was obviously going to lead nowhere. She knew the signs. It was precisely the way she and Noel had responded to their mother on rainy afternoons when they had asked her what they should do to pass the time. Mother would make suggestions, the twins would veto them, and ten minutes would pass in predictable frustration for all concerned.

Ethan was playing exactly the same game, because for some reason it amused him to provoke her.

She closed her eyes and let out a deliberately unladylike yawn.

'Charming tonsils,' he observed. 'You do have your good points, Ms Adams.

All right, I'll try the employment office. Sleep well.'

Holly didn't answer, but she kept her eyes closed for so long waiting for him to leave the room that before she knew it she had fallen asleep.

★ ★ ★

'Adams? Are you out of your mind?'

'No more so than usual,' replied Holly cheerfully. She propped her shoulder against the door-jamb of Ethan's office. 'I'm very bored, though, so I thought I'd see how you and Candy are doing.'

'Candy and I are doing about as well as your average cat and mouse. She's the mouse — so terrified of making a mistake that she makes dozens. And although I suspect she knows how to spell, she doesn't believe in contradicting the boss. If I spelled my own name backwards she'd let it pass.' He glared at her. 'And you ought to be in bed, Ms Adams.'

Just for a moment, as her eyes fastened on the fullness of his lips, she wondered how many women he had said that to with quite a different meaning, and with a very different end in mind.

She pushed the thought away and glanced quickly over her shoulder. Candy, a middle-aged woman with a pronounced overbite, was just returning to her desk.

'I'm not supposed to stay in bed forever.' Holly shut the door and limped her way into his office. 'It's good for me to move around.' She stood her crutches beside a black executive armchair and flopped awkwardly on to the seat.

'Did I invite you in?' asked Ethan, arching provocatively well-shaped eyebrows. 'I don't recall it.'

Oh, so that was the way the wind blew this morning. He was in one of his sarcastically patronising moods.

Three weeks had passed since the night of the accident, and she had been home from the hospital almost two. Ethan hadn't appeared again after that first visit, and Holly hadn't expected he would. On his instructions, Candy had phoned several times to check on her health, and flowers had arrived on cue three times a week. But there had been no personal contact.

She tried to tell herself she didn't mind, that he was doing all the correct things in a business-like and boss-like way. But she found she missed the office and, if she was honest, missed Ethan's despotic presence in her life. Now that she had the opportunity to get through whole days in a row without interference, interruption or downright aggravation, she didn't know what to do with her time. So she played with Chris, read every book in the house, talked endlessly on the phone, and thought about taking up tatting.

Today the first crocuses had pushed their way through the weeds in her brother's lawn. Spring scented the air, and she had been able to endure her enforced inactivity no longer. So she had hired a taxi and hobbled into the office. After half an hour spent wasting the time of her old friends in the payroll department, she had decided to give Candy a break and waste Ethan's time for him instead.

But from the look on his face she judged she had made a mistake. His words hadn't been encouraging either.

'No, you didn't invite me,' she said, still determinedly cheerful. 'Are you really having a bad time with Candy?'

'Yes. Or, to put it another way, if things don't change she'll find she's having a bad time with me.' He rested his forearms on the desk and regarded her with a look that seemed to be a mixture of irritation, amusement and speculation. 'You're taking up my time,' he said abruptly. 'Is there some purpose to this visit?'

'Yes,' said Holly glibly. 'I came to see if you'd like me to come back now instead of next month. But since you're having such fun tormenting Candy — '

'I am not having fun tormenting Candy, but I can see myself having enormous fun tormenting you. OK. Come back if you're up to it.'

Just like that. Holly eyed the large brass ashtray on his desk and allowed herself a moment's exquisite pleasure imagining the dent it would make in his head. Then she relinquished the fancy reluctantly and reminded herself that she was easygoing Holly Adams who always conducted herself with dignity and good sense.

'Thank you for your enthusiastic permission,' she said drily. 'On second thoughts — '

Ethan held up his hand. 'No. Let's start again, shall we? No second thoughts permitted. Holly Adams, I would love you to save my sanity and come back. I don't believe I can survive another day without you. How was that? Better?' He sat back, looking pleased with himself.

'What? You can't survive . . . ? Oh, I see. You mean in the office.' Holly swallowed.

Ethan stared at her, a small groove between his heavy eyebrows. 'Of course. You surely didn't think — ?'

'Certainly not,' she said quickly, twisting her fingers in her lap. What on earth had made her say that? She'd known perfectly well he meant he needed her in the office. In her case, men never meant anything else. Nor did she expect or want them to. Life was much pleasanter if one's dreams were grounded in reality, as hers were: a small home of her own, a bit of a garden, and two cats. In ten years she could very well have those things. In twenty years people would be referring to her as 'that funny old biddy with the cats'.

Holly shivered suddenly, grabbed her crutches, and stumbled on to her feet.

Ethan stood up and helped her to the door.

'Candy,' said Holly. 'What about — ?'

'Don't worry. I'll handle Candy. Pay in lieu of work is very effective. You'll be in tomorrow, I hope?'

She nodded.

Yes, she'd be in tomorrow. But if he expected her to serve coffee, tidy his office or go shopping for him he would soon discover his error. Broken bones occasionally came in useful.

But the next morning when she arrived at work she almost fell off her crutches.

A freshly brewed mug of coffee sat on her blotter and a huge bouquet of roses decorated the centre of her desk. Ethan, smiling complacently, sat perched on a corner of it, swinging an elegant leg.

'Welcome back, Holly,' he said, taking her arm and pulling out her chair. 'If you need anything, just let me know.'

Holly gaped at him. Surely he hadn't been drinking? She sniffed discreetly. No, just the usual spicy, masculine scent that she'd come to associate with Ethan. She sniffed again. She hadn't realised how much she'd missed that delectable odour.

'Are you all right?' she asked doubtfully.

'Never better. Can I sharpen your pencils for you? Get you more stationery, or fresh coffee . . . ?'

Holly shook her head. His hands were massaging her shoulders, and they felt firm and warm and very nice. A feeling she had never experienced before began to percolate mysteriously through her body and she restrained a crazy urge to start purring like a kitten.

He paused for a moment in his ministrations, and she turned to look up at him and smile. Their eyes met, and she saw his face change suddenly and go very still.

Her smile faded. What had happened? Why was he looking at her as if he'd just seen a very unwelcome ghost? She wriggled uncomfortably, and at once he put his hands on the sides of her head and turned it so that she was facing away from him. Then he resumed his massage as if he were dealing with recalcitrant bread dough.

Holly stared straight ahead, enjoying his expert touch, but confused and puzzled. What *had* happened just then? Because something had.

In the end, she decided Ethan must have gone temporarily mad. But it was a pleasant madness, and it was beginning to make her feel all soft and lethargic. If only it would last . . .

Of course it wouldn't, but she might as well make the most of it while it did.

She was right. Ethan's unprecedented thoughtfulness lasted for precisely one hour before she heard his voice roaring into the telephone. Which was surprising. He didn't usually roar except at his sister, Ellen, and that, she suspected, was more out of habit than bad temper.

One minute later he was standing in front of her, pounding her desk with his fist.

'Right,' said Holly calmly. 'What have I done?'

'What have *you* done? You haven't done anything yet as far as I know. And I hope you don't intend to, because I've had about enough of air-headed, flighty women for one day.'

'I am not,' said Holly coldly, 'either air-headed or remotely flighty. And if you don't behave civilly, Mr Yorke, I may have to take the rest of my sick leave after all.'

'Oh, no.' Ethan took a deep breath and wiped the back of a hand across his forehead. 'Don't try it, Holly, or, I warn you, *I* may find I have to give you reason to take it.'

'Oh? How?' asked Holly, tapping her fingers on the desk.

He fixed her with a forbidding brown eye. 'I could start by sacking you.'

Holly stared at the skin stretched tight around his jawline, and she bit her lip. 'That *would* solve your problem, wouldn't it?' she remarked mildly.

'No, but it would certainly improve my temper.' He regarded her in silence for a while, then added with a rueful shrug, 'On the other hand, I'd prefer to take it out on Ellen. My sister has a remarkable talent for driving me crazy.'

'So I've noticed.'

'Oh, you have, have you? In that case perhaps you've also noticed I have a problem — and that you're exactly the woman I need to solve it for me.'

'No,' said Holly warily. 'I haven't noticed that. What problem?'

'Ellen promised to act as my hostess at a reception I'm giving for some of our more important business contacts. Next month. My father used to do it once a year, and I've decided to carry on the tradition. Ellen, bless her pointed ears, quite cheerfully volunteered to help. But now it seems she has a new boyfriend who wants to take her to Majorca in April. As far as she's concerned, that's much more important than some dreary company reception. Which leaves me with no hostess and no one to take care of the arrangements.'

'Oh,' said Holly. 'Er — Diane Darcy?'

Ethan shook his head. 'Diane Darcy is history. We enjoyed each other's company while it lasted, but Diane has marriage on her mind. I haven't.'

'I see.'

'I'm glad you do. Because I intend for you to replace Ellen.'

Holly pushed her glasses up her nose. 'Who did you say is to replace Ellen?' she asked blankly. 'Do I know her?'

Ethan's lips parted in an unexpected but very determined grin. 'We're both in trouble if you don't. I said *you*, my efficient but unassuming assistant. *You're* going to be my hostess, Holly Adams.'

4

Holly stared up at Ethan. He was wearing an odd little half-smile, but the dark gaze fixed on her face was not accommodating. He was *telling* her what he wanted, not asking. And it didn't make any sense.

'What are you talking about?' she demanded, her tone more acidic than she'd intended.

'I'm talking about you, my splendidly capable and very estimable assistant with the impressive organisational skills. Surely that's not so hard to take in.'

He was still smiling, and his voice stroked over her like velvet. But she had a feeling that the velvet sheathed a blade.

She swallowed, and then swallowed again. There was something very persuasive about Ethan when he meant to have his way. And she had no doubt he meant to have it now.

'I *could* organise your reception,' she agreed reluctantly. 'I do see that you have a problem. But I can't possibly act as your hostess. I have a cast on my leg, and, in any case, I'm wrong for the part.'

'Your cast will be off by that time. And even if it isn't, you're exactly right for the part.'

Help! thought Holly. Her leg started to hurt and she bent down to massage it. He really meant it. But surely even he could see . . .

'I don't fit the corporate image,' she said desperately, wincing as her hand hit the cast. 'I'm just not suitable. You need someone striking, like Diane Darcy. Or your sister . . . '

'Holly,' Ethan said very softly, 'if I hear one more word about how unremarkable you are, I'll be very inclined to turn you around and administer a swift kick in the right place. I don't give a damn what you look like, and I'm getting very tired of all this rubbish about corporate images and suitability. Now — I've told you I want you for my hostess. It's part of your job. You will, therefore, do as I say and be polite and charming to my guests — who will naturally be delighted with you. Do you understand me?' He bent over her, his eyes glittering a message that for a moment was more than just a boss telling his assistant what to do. There was a gentle menace in that look. And yet it spoke to her as a man might speak to a woman he . . .

She gasped as an unexpected excitement snaked inside her, and she wondered why she suddenly felt hot.

Ethan's breath feathered over her hair, and she knew he was issuing a challenge. Did he want her to fight him, then? There was something about his stance that made her think he might appreciate a fight.

Her breath caught in her throat. No. She wasn't going to fight him. Because he was right. He had confidence in her, and there was no reason why she shouldn't have confidence in herself. If he wanted her to stand beside him on an important occasion, she would do it. With pride and — she stole a glance at his face — maybe just a little apprehension.

'Well?' His dark eyebrows slanted upwards.

'Yes,' said Holly, with a smile of overplayed meekness. 'I understand perfectly, Mr Yorke.'

Ethan nodded, and smiled back with a certain implacability. Then he straightened his spine and stepped back. 'Good,' he said evenly. 'I'm glad you've decided to see sense. And if you should feel the slightest urge to go into your wallflower routine again, Ms Adams, just remember where I said I'd place that kick.'

'You'd be up on an assault charge if you tried it,' remarked Holly. 'I'm still on crutches, remember.'

'Yes, and you could be on them for a lot longer if I hear any more nonsense about your suitability. Got that?'

'Yes, sir,' said Holly demurely. 'I'm properly terrified.'

Ethan shook his head. 'Would that you were,' he said gloomily. 'It would make my life considerably simpler. Never mind, I'll keep working on it. And meanwhile I'll introduce you to my sister before she retreats to Majorca for her holiday filled with sun and safe sex. She can give you some tips.'

'On safe sex?' asked Holly, before she could stop herself. Then she stared at him, horrified, as a sudden and utterly unforeseen vision of a beach, bright sunshine and Ethan's naked limbs sprawled beneath a cloudless blue sky invaded her mind and nearly knocked her off her chair.

Ethan cocked an eyebrow at an improbable angle, and for one horrible moment she wondered if he'd read her thoughts.

'Very probably, if you think you'd find it useful,' he drawled. 'I'm afraid that from a brother's point of view

Ellen's behaviour leaves a lot to be desired. She was always spoiled, and if she fancied something she got it. At the moment her fancies run to men. Highly ineligible men.' The eyebrows rose even higher. 'But the fact is, you mistook my meaning, my dear. I was referring to tips on organising company functions.'

'Yes,' said Holly, raising her eyes with an effort and winning the battle not to turn into a lobster. 'I did realise that. And I'd very much like to meet your sister.'

'Good.' He reversed the calendar on her desk and started flipping through the pages. 'Sunday. Come for lunch. I'll make sure Ellen stays home.'

'Home?' said Holly. 'You mean — ?'

'I mean the place Ellen calls 'the family mausoleum'. Heronwater.'

'Oh,' said Holly, trying not to look overawed. Everyone at Smart and Yorke's knew about Heronwater, the Yorkes' country estate beside the Thames. Ethan's grandfather was reputed to have won it in a poker game. It was the sort of place the average impoverished duke could never afford to keep up. The Yorkes appeared to take its maintenance in their stride.

'Well? Is Sunday all right?' demanded Ethan, breaking rudely into her thoughts. ''Oh' isn't a satisfactory answer.'

'Yes,' said Holly. 'Sunday's fine.'

He nodded, rapped his knuckles on her desk, and swung back into his office, humming a flat little tune beneath his breath.

Holly, staring after him, was left to wonder if she'd bitten off a whole lot more than she could chew.

On the other side of the wall, Ethan wiped a handkerchief round the back of his neck, and wondered why God had seen fit to create women. First Ellen, with her airy disregard for the firm's commitments, and then Holly, with her nonsense about corporate images. It was more than a man should have to put up with. Except that he needed Holly, and he had no doubt that she could handle the assignment.

Frowning, he slouched over to the

window and glared at the pale sun glancing off the dome of St Paul's. Dammit, Holly's nondescript looks were part of the reason he had hired her. If she'd been the raving beauty she seemed to imagine he favoured, there was no way he would have offered her the job. He'd had more than enough of beauty raving around his office.

He strummed his fingers on the sill. No, Holly wasn't beautiful, but she wasn't entirely unattractive. And he found her restful. She argued with him, of course, and told him how to behave. But she was efficient, she saw to his needs, and there wasn't the remotest likelihood that she would ever look on him as a ticket to a better way of life. That was why he had practically bullied her into acting as his hostess. There was no danger that she would read more into the situation than he intended. And as long as she looked neat, and performed with her usual ability, there was no reason why anything should go wrong.

Suddenly a shaft of sunlight cast a bright beam across his eyes and brought with it a memory from the past.

It had been springtime then too, and he had asked a woman he had met in Canada to help him host a company affair. Not his secretary, who was a married mother of three, but a pretty creature he'd collected at a party. She had immediately assumed she was in line to be the next Mrs Yorke, at which point she'd been ejected from his life so fast that she hadn't even had time to say, 'I love you'. If she had said it, he wouldn't have believed her. No, there would not be a repeat of that disaster. Not with Holly.

He brushed a hand over his jaw and gazed pensively at the surrounding rooftops. Then he shrugged and moved briskly to his desk to pick up the phone.

After speaking succinctly into the mouthpiece for a few seconds, he hung up, reached for a pen, and circled a date on his calendar in red.

But on Sunday, the date in question, when he arrived at Holly's home to pick her up, he was told that she had gone for a walk on Chiswick Common.

'She can't have,' he said to an embarrassed Barbara, who stood in the doorway fidgeting with the collar of her blouse. 'For one thing, she can't walk. For another, she's having lunch with me.'

'Yes, I know. She was all ready to go, and then about half an hour ago she suddenly said she needed some air. Noel said you'd be here any minute, but that only sent her scurrying for her crutches. And it's true she can't exactly walk, but she can certainly swing.' Ethan scowled at her, and Barbara added quickly, 'I'm sorry. You can probably find her on the common.' She started on the other point of the collar.

'Thank you,' said Ethan grimly. 'Don't worry, I'll find her.'

He saw Barbara's eyes widen before he strode off down the path, feeling a lot like a truant officer in pursuit of an errant child — a child whose ears he would very much like to box severely. And if Barbara was afraid he would do her sister-in-law harm in his current mood, she wasn't very far off the mark.

He saw Holly before she saw him. She was hunched on a bench beneath some trees. Her crutches were propped beside her, and she seemed oblivious to the chill. She reminded Ethan of a neglected mushroom in her grey coat and soft felt beret.

'What the devil do you mean by running away on me?' he asked, in a voice which he tried unsuccessfully to keep level. 'I don't like being stood up.'

She gasped, and he saw her hands clench on her knees before she raised her golden eyes to his with a look that was defiant and contrite, but not afraid.

'I wasn't running away,' she said quietly. 'I just realised I needed time to think.

'If you mean you had to think about whether you were going to have lunch with me, you've already had four days.

Common courtesy should have prompted you to let me know that you intended to change the game plan.'

'I *didn't* intend to.'

Ethan was not altogether surprised to feel his control snap like a taut rubber band. Dammit; obliging, sensible Holly Adams had no business to lead him on such a dance. This was the sort of trick his sister pulled. But not Holly. And if she thought she was going to get away with it, she was wrong.

'Right,' he said, taking her arm and hauling her on to her one usable foot. 'There will be no more of this silliness, Holly. My family are expecting us for lunch and if we don't get a move on we'll be late. My father doesn't take kindly to tardiness and neither do I.' He picked up her crutches with one hand and shoved them at her. Then he put his other hand in the small of her back and said, 'Hustle.'

She hustled.

★ ★ ★

Holly leaned as far away from Ethan as possible — if the door of the car had opened suddenly she would have ended up on the road — and gazed glumly at the stern set of his jaw above the neckline of his black polo-neck sweater. She supposed that was his idea of casual Sunday attire, but in fact it made him look rather more of a dangerous powerhouse than usual.

She couldn't blame him for being angry. It had been sheer cowardice that had driven her on to the common. Sheer rudeness too. And she *had*, in a sense, been running away. She hadn't meant it to happen, but as she'd sat at the kitchen table sipping coffee and waiting for him a few drops had fallen on her dress. When she'd gone to wipe them up, all at once she had become aware of just how ordinary she must look in her inexpensive black dress with the cultured pearls: a dumpy little crow with a broken ankle, on her way to have lunch with a prince who had never been turned into a frog.

All her doubts had come crashing in on her again, and over Barbara's and Noel's protests she had seized her coat and the grey beret and hurtled out on to the street. Almost immediately instinct had directed her to the common, where she always found peace when she needed to be alone to think. At the beginning of March there were not many people about, and her favourite bench had been vacant.

But when she had tried to get her thoughts in order, an insistent voice in her mind kept telling her that this wasn't a time for thinking, it was a time for doing. As in going straight back to the house to fulfill her commitment to Ethan. He had never complained about her undistinguished clothes before, so he wasn't likely to start on them now. She doubted if he even noticed what she wore. A lot of men didn't. Not even ones who had made their fortunes out of women's clothing. In any case, she had never cared much when men noticed since the day Andy refused to take her to the dance, and she had seen him kissing the greengrocer's daughter. Even though that old and painful wound had healed, not caring had somehow become a habit.

Just when she had reached the conclusion that her unusual attack of panic was over, and that she had better heave herself home at once, Ethan's voice had broken over her like avenging thunder. The next thing she knew, she was being steamrollered down the path and into his newly repaired car.

He still wore a thunderous expression, but she knew him well enough now to believe he had the worst of the storm under control. And she had never been afraid of him physically. It was his position, and the things he stood for, that occasionally put a dent in her confidence.

'I'm sorry,' she ventured. 'I shouldn't have left when I did.'

'No, you shouldn't. And I hope you're not going to indulge in any more vapours over this damned reception, because if you are I'll have to replace you. I engaged you to be reliable, Holly, not irresponsible.'

His words cut through her like a lash, but she managed to lift up her chin and say calmly, 'I wasn't indulging in vapours. I promised to do the job and I will. But if you're having second thoughts, I won't blame you. Naturally, if you think someone else would suit you better — '

'Yes, I know: you will step meekly and obligingly aside. What is it with you, Holly? You have no problem telling me how to run my office, but, when it comes to the outside world, all of a sudden you turn into jelly. Did your parents teach you that ladies are supposed to be docile and self-effacing, and beat all the spunk out of you whenever you rebelled? Which I'd be willing to bet you often did.'

Holly sighed. 'Not that often. And no, they didn't beat me, although my father did have a temper. Mother was very patient and tried to explain why

118

rebelling wouldn't get me what I wanted.'

'And what did you want?'

'Oh, the usual things: a palace, Prince Charming, a Rolls-Royce. My parents suggested I go for some solid business training and learn to support myself instead.' She twisted the pearls at her neck. 'They didn't hold out much hope of a Prince Charming coming along to do it for me — said I wasn't the type to attract princes, and anyway, I should learn to stand on my own feet. After Andy deserted me, I began to see that they'd been right.'

'Hmm.' Ethan stared straight ahead at the steeple of a small village church. 'Every woman should learn to support herself, but that doesn't mean she can't have a life. And that doesn't necessarily mean princes. You must have been a very confused child.'

'Oh, I don't know. I was happy enough. Noel got most of the attention, mainly because he demanded it, but I never minded that. He and I were always close, being twins. Even more so after Mother and Dad died.'

'You're young to have lost both your parents.'

It was a straight statement of fact, and because he didn't offer meaningless sympathy, Holly was able to reply quite calmly. 'Yes. Mum died suddenly of pneumonia. Dad didn't care much after that. He crashed his car three months later.'

'Suicide?'

Still no sympathy. Just a question. He seemed to understand instinctively that pity was the one thing that might cause her to break down.

She shook her head. 'No, they didn't think so. He just didn't care enough to take care. Noel and I were only seventeen. It happened just before the end of school.' And just before I lost Andy, were the words she left unsaid. But she suspected Ethan had made the connection when unexpectedly he reached across to pat her knee.

She started, and began to draw away,

but his hand was already back on the wheel.

'We moved in with a neighbour for a few months,' she finished a little breathlessly. 'Then we both came to London to find jobs.'

'Where you, at least, have kept your head down and your nose commendably glued to Smart and Yorke's grindstone. Yes, I do begin to see why you make such a satisfactory assistant — and such a damned unsatisfactory everything else.'

Holly's mouth opened, then snapped shut. She hadn't wanted sympathy, and she hadn't got it. If he meant that her natural reticence, combined with the sudden death of her parents and the loss of Andy, had turned her into an unsatisfactory woman filled with self-doubt . . . well, he could just go on thinking that. She had no doubts about her ability to run an office, which was all that was important to her. It ought to be all that was important to him.

Ethan flicked a quick glance at the

indignant angle of her chin, and said evenly, 'All right, I shouldn't have said that. And if you really don't want to be my hostess, Holly, you know you only have to say so.'

'That wasn't the impression I formed the other day,' she muttered. 'I seem to remember being told it was part of the job.'

'That's better,' said Ethan.

'What is?'

'You're arguing with me again. Now then, Ms Adams . . . ' He drew the car close to the hedge at the side of a winding Surrey lane. 'Have we quite finished with the nonsense? Or do you want to back out while you can?'

Holly turned to stare out of the window. Thank heavens he'd had the perception, or maybe just the plain self-interest, to let go of the painful subject of her past and get back to the matter in hand. And no, she thought dazedly. No, damn him, I don't want to back out.

There was something about Ethan that inspired confidence, in spite of, or perhaps because of, his cool assumption that whatever he'd decided on must be right. And there was no reason she couldn't do as he wanted. She'd had one brief and unexpected attack of trepidation, but it was over. There wouldn't be any more.

'I'd like to keep my promise,' she told him, straightening her spine against the seat. 'I'm sorry about the silliness. It won't happen again.'

'Good girl.'

Quite suddenly, as Holly sat with her hands in her lap, staring at a couple of cows mooing mournfully in a mud-brown field, she felt Ethan's hand on her chin. When he turned her to face him she saw that his eyes were warm with something that might almost be understanding.

'Good girl,' he said again, patting her cheek. 'With a little effort, you know, you and I could get along with each other very well.'

'In what way?' asked Holly doubt-fully. She found herself liking the firm touch of his fingers on her skin, but it disturbed her too, and she didn't altogether know why.

Ethan frowned. 'As a working team, of course,' he replied, as though there could be no other answer. He dropped his hand abruptly, switched on the engine, and pulled into the road a bit too fast.

Holly bit her lip. Nothing had happened, and yet in some obscure way she felt she had lost something — something she had never really had.

Ten minutes later Ethan pulled the car onto a long beech-lined driveway. Leafless branches stood out nakedly against the washed-out blue of the sky. At the very end of the driveway stood a sturdy, E-shaped manor house. It was built of red brick mellowed by centuries of unpredictable English weather. The two wings were both adorned by Elizabethan turrets. As they drew closer to the house, Holly saw that well-kept lawns swept down like swatches of green velvet to the river.

124

'Heronwater,' said Ethan, as they came to a stop in the courtyard in the centre of the E. 'Ellen's mausoleum.'

'But it's beautiful,' exclaimed Holly. 'Do . . . do just the three of you live here?'

'In plutocratic state? Not exactly. We employ a staff, Ellen stocks the place with her lame ducks and hangers-on when she's in residence, and the west wing is used as a nursing home for recovering stroke patients.'

Yes, Holly had heard rumours of the Yorkes' philanthropic activities. She just hadn't realised that they encouraged them this close to home.

The front door swung open to reveal a high-ceilinged hallway supported by weathered oak beams. Holly glanced up, expecting to see a butler or some such intimidating being, but Colby Yorke stood in the entrance, upright and elegant despite his lined face and smooth white hair.

'Ah. Miss Adams.' He came up to the car and held out his hand. 'I believe we've met . . . ' His voice trailed off, and Holly knew he didn't remember her at all from the years when they had spent every day in the same building. He was also surprised by the cast on her leg. Had Ethan forgotten to tell him?

'Yes,' she said brightly, accepting the proffered hand. 'But of course you couldn't possibly remember all the staff.' She refrained from mentioning that Ethan already knew each employee by name. He sometimes muddled them, but he knew them.

Colby Yorke ushered them across the hall and into a small, sunlit sitting room with tall lead-paned windows overlooking a wild country garden. Across the room a comfortable fire was burning inside a terracotta fireplace embossed with the original owner's coat of arms. It threw a welcome blanket of heat over the new arrivals. Holly had been reluctant to relinquish her coat in the draughty hallway, until Ethan had removed it with a polite but unyielding smile. Now she was glad she had not resisted too strongly.

Careful not to get in the way of her crutches, he led her across a deep red oriental carpet to a high-backed chair beside the hearth. She sat down, and Colby brought her a sherry.

'So, Miss Adams,' he said, settling into a chair directly opposite, and running what she supposed was meant to be a discreet eye over her face and figure, 'my son tells me you're handling the firm's reception for him next month.'

His cold blue gaze told Holly that he was by no means impressed with Ethan's choice.

'Yes,' she replied coolly. 'I do hope it will be a success.'

'It always has been,' said Colby, in a tone that indicated he had grave doubts of the reception's chances this year.

Ethan settled himself on a satin love-seat and crossed his legs. 'Where's Ellen?' he asked his father.

'Feeding the ducks.'

'Human or feathered?'

'Feathered, thank goodness. The last lot of lame ones left yesterday — two sisters who appeared for dinner wearing ugly little numbers made of sacking.' Colby shook his head. 'Seems they're trying to make a living painting what they call 'interpretative' portraits of people's dogs. Thing is, people don't want their dogs interpreted. Why should they? Anyway, Ellen felt sorry for them. You know Ellen.' He smiled fondly, and Holly guessed that in her father's eyes, at least, his unconventional daughter could do no wrong.

'Yes,' said Ethan heavily. 'I know Ellen. Is the new boyfriend with her?'

'Gone back to town. Just as well. Fellow wears a ponytail. And an earring.'

'He would,' muttered Ethan.

Holly smiled into her sherry. It was apparent that Ethan did not share his father's tolerance of Ellen's eccentricities. It was also apparent, from the glare that Colby threw at his son, that criticism of the daughter of the house was a privilege reserved for her father. Probably she was also the favoured child.

For the first time that she could remember, Holly found herself feeling a little sorry for Ethan. She knew his mother had died when he was very young, and that he had been packed off to boarding-school at an early age while his sister had remained in the family home. Probably he had felt unwanted a lot of the time. And there were rumours of some scandal soon after he'd entered the firm.

These days he was self-assured to the point of arrogance, but maybe it had not always been so.

He gave her a small smile and lifted his glass. Holly smiled back, and when their eyes met in wary understanding she felt an unexpected glow of warmth.

Lunch, in the long, narrow dining-room with its carved ebony table that must have been there almost as long as the house, might have been a nerve-racking affair. But it wasn't, because just as a tall, solemn-faced butler appeared, bearing a silver tray laden with covered dishes — Holly had been sure there was a butler somewhere — a commotion started up in the doorway and a high-pitched, girlish voice trilled, 'Sorry I'm late, Daddy. One of the ducks got caught in some reeds and I fell in trying to disentangle it.'

'That must have been a great help to the duck,' observed Ethan.

'Oh, it was. It took one look at me floundering around covered in weeds and swam away.' Ellen lowered herself gracefully into the chair across from her father.

Holly, waiting to be introduced, saw a thin, fine-boned young woman with closely cropped fair hair and a patrician nose. Now, dressed in a flowing white dress that would have been better suited to July, she showed no sign of her untimely dunking. She smiled sweetly at Holly and said, 'You must be Ethan's right-hand woman. He says you didn't want to take over the reception, but you've agreed to do it. You shouldn't have, you know. He gets his own way far too much.'

'Not with you, I don't,' said Ethan grimly.

Ellen shrugged. 'Somebody has to keep you in line.'

'Hmm. I strongly suspect Holly agrees with you,' murmured Ethan, helping himself to the potatoes and vegetables being offered by the solemn-faced butler.

'Good,' said Ellen. 'Then she won't let you walk all over her. Are you really going to run the reception, Holly? It's an awful bore.'

'Oh, come, now,' said Colby. 'You've only done it once, my dear, and everyone said you were a charming hostess. I really think it would be much more satisfactory if this year — '

'Holly is doing it this year,' said Ethan shortly. 'She'll do just as well.'

'Hmm,' Colby grunted, and cast a dubious look at Holly over his wine glass.

Somehow she got through the meal without committing any of the social gaffes she'd been afraid of making, but, in spite of Ellen's bubbling chatter and goodwill, she couldn't avoid knowing that Colby Yorke remained unconvinced of her ability to handle the reception. Earlier, she would have been half inclined to agree with him. Now it merely served to stiffen her resolve to do the job.

After lunch Ellen put her arm through Holly's and said it was time they got down to business. When Ethan attempted to follow, Ellen told him to go away and not interfere.

'Considering the firm's paying for this shindig, I think I have every right to interfere.' Ethan gave his sister a superior smile which seemed not to faze her a bit.

'No, you haven't. You'll only make Holly nervous.'

'Hmm.' The smile disappeared, and he cast a quick, appraising glance at Holly's face. But in the end he turned away and strode off down the passage with his hands rammed into the pockets of his trousers.

Holly looked up at Ellen ruefully. 'I don't know how you did that, but I wish *I* could.' She sighed. 'And you're right in a way. It's not that he makes me nervous exactly, but he's very . . . well . . . '

'Interfering and bossy,' said Ellen. 'We'll do a lot better without him.'

Soon the two of them were ensconced in Ellen's pretty sitting-room, deep in caterers' brochures, guest lists and menus. Holly discovered almost at once that, although Ellen had a reputation for flightiness, she was a lot more capable than she let on. As Ethan well knew, or he wouldn't have asked her to be his hostess.

'Are you and Ethan serious about each other?' asked Ellen bluntly, when the last brochure had been stowed away and they were making their way back to join the men. 'I didn't think he had that much good sense.'

'Oh, no.' Holly was aghast and embarrassed. 'I'm just his assistant.'

'Oh.' Ellen made a face. 'I might have known. Listen, Holly, I like you, and I'm sorry I've let you in for this business. But you do see . . . I mean Boyd, my boyfriend, wouldn't understand about company parties . . . '

'Don't apologise,' said Holly quickly. 'I'm beginning to see it as a challenge.'

'Oh, it will be.' Ellen rolled her eyes up. 'Loads of lecherous men using their mid-life crisis as an excuse to grope you. The biggest challenge will be avoiding their roaming hands.'

Holly took in Ellen's svelte figure, and aristocratic model's face. 'I don't think I'll have that problem,' she said drily, as she clumped along beside her new friend.

'Don't count on it,' muttered Ellen. 'Listen, I'm off to join Boyd in about an hour and I still have some packing to do. Can you find your own way back to Ethan? Or do you need some help?'

'I'm fine,' said Holly. 'I'm getting

pretty used to these crutches.'

'Sure?'

Holly was sure, and a few moments later she was leaning against the wall as she reached for the handle of the door into the sitting room with the fire.

'She'll never be able to handle it, for heaven's sake. She's too quiet, and she doesn't even look like a hostess.'

Colby's voice came to Holly through the door like a bucket of ice thrown at her face. She froze with her hand on the handle.

'And what does a hostess look like?' Ethan's controlled drawl was pitched lower than his father's, but it was still audible.

'Well — like your aunt Julia. She, at least, had dignity and distinction.'

'She's also dead. Has been for two years. What do you suggest I do, Dad? Tie Ellen up by the hair and destroy her ticket to Majorca? I grant you it might do her a lot of good. Might do me some good too.'

'There's no need to be unkind about

your sister. She's young. Of course she wants a bit of fun.'

'Is that what you call it? I could think of another word to describe what Ellen wants. In any case, Holly's my best bet.'

'But she looks like . . . like a . . . '

'Mushroom. Yes, I know. Nevertheless, I have faith in her, and . . . '

Holly didn't hear any more. So that was how Ethan saw her: as a mushroom in whom he had faith. And his father didn't even have that. It would serve them both right if she backed out right now and told them they could find someone else.

But she wasn't going to. Holly's lips tightened. No, she was not going to roll over and play dead just because two arrogant men had made heartless and unflattering comments about her appearance.

She was going to accept the challenge and she was going to go right in there and confront them.

Heaving herself away from the wall, Holly pushed open the door with a crutch and hopped her way into the room.

5

'Greetings from the mushroom,' murmured Holly, as she dropped into the nearest chair.

Colby, who had been standing beside the hearth, bent down and made a great production of stoking up the already roaring fire.

Ethan, who was seated, stood up and took a half-step towards her. For a few seconds his face registered consternation — which changed almost at once to amusement.

'I happen to like mushrooms,' he remarked, gazing blandly at the dark beams of the ceiling.

'Sure. Especially ones that lack dignity and distinction.'

Colby cleared his throat, and Ethan stopped studying the ceiling and looked directly into her eyes. 'I didn't say that. And I hope you don't plan to use my father's unfortunate remark as an excuse to back out of your commitment.'

'Certainly not,' said Holly. 'As a matter of fact the two of you have convinced me I made the right decision.'

Ethan's mouth curved into a sceptical grimace. 'Does that mean I ought to be quaking in my boots? I'm told revenge can be a great source of inspiration.'

'Can it? I'd love to see you quake,' said Holly, who couldn't imagine anything less likely.

The grimace became positively malignant. 'I wouldn't get your hopes up,' he drawled.

Colby looked up from the fire, which was beginning to show signs of fighting back. 'Miss Adams,' he said, swallowing with obvious embarrassment, 'I sincerely regret that you overheard what I said to my son. Of course both of us believe you will do your best, but you should understand — '

'I do,' said Holly, smiling sweetly.

She did too. Ethan's words had

brought home to Colby the possibility that a deeply offended and reasonably intelligent mushroom could very easily wreak havoc on the firm's reception — should she be so inclined.

'Yes, well . . . ' Colby cleared his throat again. 'I'm — er — glad you do. And — er — my apologies. I'm sure you'll do very well.' He muttered the last sentence very fast, as if he was afraid that if he didn't speak quickly he would be unable to enunciate the lie.

Ethan said nothing. He had his hands in his pockets again and was looking down at Holly with an expression she found hard to interpret. At first she thought it might be pity, but his mouth was quirked at an angle that she normally associated with derision. And that black sweater pulling tight across his chest made him look dangerous, not sympathetic.

'Of course I'll do my best, Mr Yorke,' said Holly evenly. 'Ethan, I think it's time I went home.'

'So do I,' said Ethan, with an

unflattering alacrity that brought home to her just how much his careless cruelty had, and was continuing to, hurt. To her horror, she felt tears prick the back of her eyes.

She thought Ethan must have seen them, because he said in a much softer voice, 'Come along, then,' and held out his hand.

Holly took it, and he pulled her on to her feet. To her surprise and confusion, she felt an unaccustomed tingling in her palm, and she brushed it hastily down the side of her dress.

The drive home was silent and, from Holly's point of view, uncomfortable. Somehow she had the feeling that Ethan was blaming her for having overheard him, rather than himself and his father for saying those unforgivable things.

When they came to a stop outside her house, she decided to confirm her impression.

'I suppose you think I shouldn't have been outside that door,' she said stiffly.

'Well, you had to be outside it at some point. Of course I would have preferred it if you'd come straight in, instead of pausing to listen. In any case, my dear Ms Adams, I meant it when I said I had faith in you. I also meant it when I told you I like mushrooms.' He shifted round on the seat, and fixed her with an imperious brown eye. 'And let me assure you, just in case you have any ideas, that if you think of sabotaging Smart and Yorke's arrangements I will personally see to it that you won't want to do it again.'

'Ooh,' said Holly, blinking bravely from behind her glasses. 'Are you going to go all macho on me, Ethan? How exciting.'

'Cut it out, Adams,' he said roughly. 'Believe me, if you mess up deliberately, you'll get a lot more excitement than you need.'

Holly stared at him. His large hands rested on his thighs and he was scowling at a passing vicar as if he'd very much like to punch him on the nose. And it occurred to her that he wasn't nearly as angry with her as he was with himself. It was also possible that he genuinely thought she might try to ruin his plans — which was a lot worse than being called a mushroom.

'Ethan,' she said wearily, 'I don't particularly mind being thought of as an edible fungus. But I do mind the suggestion that I'm the kind of woman who would purposely set out to damage the firm which has employed her for the past five years.' She reached for the handle. 'Thank you for lunch. I'll see you at work tomorrow.'

In an instant Ethan was out of the car and swinging open her door. 'OK,' he said, as he helped her out, 'I admit I had no business to suggest you were that sort of woman. Now all you have to do is prove to me that you're not.' He gave her a challenging smile and tucked a loose strand of hair behind her ear.

As if I'm his little sister being tidied up for school, thought Holly resentfully.

And yet there was something undeniably intimate about the gesture . . .

She frowned, and contemplated hitting him over the head with a crutch, but decided it wouldn't do much to soothe the wounds he'd so carelessly inflicted. Besides, the way things were going today, she'd probably end up flat on her face.

'I don't have to prove anything to you,' she said coolly. 'I do, however, have something to prove to myself.' Lifting her chin proudly, she turned to swing herself up the pathway to the house.

Ethan came up behind her. Holly wished she knew what was really going on in his mind, but as he was obviously in one of his Lord of the Universe humours she felt no inclination to ask him in. Nor did he seem to expect an invitation.

She said goodbye, he murmured a polite reply, and by the time she had her coat off and went to look out of the window the Maserati was already out of sight.

The next few weeks passed quickly. A wary but more or less unarmed truce was maintained at the office, with communication kept on a strictly business basis. Plans for the reception moved smoothly ahead. Holly discovered that she enjoyed this new outlet for her organisational talents, and somewhere along the line she decided it was also time to organise herself.

Without quite knowing how it came about, she found herself eating less. Whereas before she had been quite happy to make a lunch of chocolate and cream cheese sandwiches, now she munched discreetly on carrots.

At the end of March the cast was removed from her leg, and when she looked in the mirror one evening she saw not a slim and slinky siren exactly, but a pleasantly rounded, neatly curvaceous young woman in a slightly too large amber dress.

'Wow,' exclaimed Barbara, coming into the green and white bedroom and plumping herself down on Holly's bed.

'I'd no idea you were hiding such a nice figure under all those lumpy suits of yours, Holly. Is it for Ethan?'

'No,' said Holly quickly, but quite truthfully. 'It's for me.'

'Good.' Barbara pursed her lips. 'You know, if you bought some new clothes, and got rid of these owlish glasses — '

'I happen to be blind as a bat without those glasses.

'Yes, but you could wear contacts.'

'No, I couldn't. I don't like the idea of taking my eyes in and out.'

'Well, all right, but you don't *have* to look like an owl.'

Holly sighed. 'I don't. Ethan says I look like a mushroom.'

'Ethan's an idiot,' said Barbara.

'No, just a man. As in annoying, opinionated and smug.'

Barbara shook her head and went away muttering something about bats not being the only ones who were blind, and Holly sat down in front of her dressing-table to study the glasses that were the cause of the dissension.

Two days later she visited the local optician and ordered a pair of emerald-green cat's-eye frames that she was informed by the clerk who served her were out of fashion.

Holly didn't care. They made her rounded face look almost oval, and the green enhanced the colour of her eyes. Even her skin no longer looked as if it had been washed and bleached before being hung out to dry.

Then, deciding she might as well go the whole way, she took a deep breath and paid a visit to a well-known boutique whose exclusive portals she had always given a wide berth up till now.

★ ★ ★

Ethan seemed preoccupied on the evening of the Smart and Yorke reception. He hardly spoke a word as he drove Holly to the Mayfair hotel she had selected as the most suitable to the occasion, and she didn't think he had even noticed her appearance. Not that

146

there was anything new in that.

But when he helped her off with her coat she felt his fingers tighten on her shoulders, and suddenly he was swinging her around.

'Well, I'll be damned,' he murmured, his eyes raking over her as no man's eyes had ever done before. 'Where have you been hiding the fairy godmother, Holly?'

'What do you mean?' asked Holly, who had a pretty fair idea what he meant, and didn't much like being compared to Cinderella.

'You're thinner, your hair looks brighter — '

'It's a rinse.'

Ethan ignored her. 'And you are wearing glasses that actually suit your face, as well as a dress that bears no resemblance to a tepee.' He shook his head, and she had an odd feeling he wasn't altogether pleased.

'Do you approve?' she asked lightly, surprised to find herself hanging on his answer.

'Sure. Why shouldn't I?' He removed his hands abruptly, took her arm, and began to march her much too quickly down the hall.

Holly felt a familiar urge to gnash her teeth. She had spent a fortune on her pale green dress with the full sleeves and the fitted bodice which, as he had so rudely pointed out, most certainly did not make her look like a tepee. It made her look like a perfectly presentable woman with a figure. And she actually felt quite attractive. Ethan had been right after all. So had Barbara. It was true that ever since Andy's desertion she had been using her looks to shield herself from hurt, instead of trying to make the most of herself.

No more. She wasn't going to do it any more — even though Ethan had just shrugged and said, 'Sure', as if she had asked him if he approved of her new umbrella.

As they entered an elegant reception-room with an expensive dove-grey carpet and pale peach walls, it did occur to Holly to wonder why his lack of enthusiasm hurt a little, but soon she was too caught up in last-minute spot checks and consultations with catering staff to have time for more personal reflections.

Then the first guests arrived, and after that she forgot about Ethan, the man, as she stood proudly beside Ethan, the president, and welcomed a steady stream of perfectly coiffed ladies accompanied by well-dressed, suavely confident men.

At least, she forgot about him until one of the men, who looked well fed as well as well dressed, came up beside her as she chatted with a group of attentive accountants and placed a moist hand on the back of her thigh.

Holly froze. Her first impulse was to slug him on the nose, but Ethan was standing across the room, being charming to a stunning brunette. Slugging a guest, and becoming the centre of a scene, wasn't likely to endear her to her boss. Nor would it do a thing for the image of the firm she had agreed to represent.

She stepped away from the smooth-faced lecher and tried to pretend she hadn't noticed. But his hand followed her, and now she felt it sliding beneath her dress.

Holly stifled a gasp, beamed brightly at the oblivious accountants, and mumbled, 'Excuse me. I have to . . . I mean, I think there's a problem with the — er — the caviare.' She darted away from the startled little group before they had a chance to respond. But when she glanced over her shoulder, she saw that the man with the hands was in hot pursuit.

Holly hesitated, not sure what she ought to do next. She wasn't used to coping with sleazy passes — and probably this smarmy creep knew it. All the same, something had to be done. Squaring her shoulders, she clutched the pearl handles of her bag, and looked hopefully around the room for a solution. Her gaze fell on a grey-haired couple who were standing neglected in a corner. She hurried over to join them and braced her back against the wall.

'Ah, Miss Adams. A most delightful party.' The creep was right beside her again, in no way distracted from his prey.

'Thank you,' said Holly, edging away.

The grey-haired couple, feeling crowded, moved back to give her more room, and at once Hands took over the vacant space. Again Holly felt plump fingers squeezing her thigh.

Discreetly she eased her arm behind her back and tried to push the fingers away. But they didn't budge, and when she looked at the man's face she was left in no doubt at all that he knew he wasn't dealing with a woman of the world, and was taking full advantage of that knowledge. He smiled, a bland smile that made Holly think of grease.

'Yes, so enjoyable . . . ' murmured the grey-haired woman, obviously puzzled by her hostess's set face and lack of conversation.

Holly made up her mind. She might be lacking in sophistication, but she wasn't that short on self-respect — and she wasn't putting up with this man's mauling for one more second. It might be nice if St George suddenly appeared to sweep through the assembled throng and slay her groping dragon with a stroke. But, unfortunately, St George was a myth.

Ethan Yorke, however, was not.

Just as Holly opened her mouth to tell Hands that if he didn't get away from her at once she would be obliged to change the shape of his nose, she caught sight of Ethan conversing with a pixie-faced girl who was gazing up at him as though she'd just seen a vision of holy matrimony complete with massed heavenly choirs.

He was twirling a glass between his fingers, but when his eyes met Holly's she saw him stiffen. Granite, she thought with a start. His face has gone harder than a rock.

Beside her, Hands made a move to

advance his position, and Holly forgot her boss and lifted her hand.

But before her aim could find its mark she discovered that Ethan, looking powerful and much larger than life, had materialised next to her tormentor. He was smiling a cat-like smile, and resting one casual fist against the wall. Holly hesitated, then lowered her arm as she heard Hands let out a gasp. His hold on her thigh loosed abruptly, and before anyone had a chance to react he had thrown a venomous glance at his host and disappeared into the crowd.

Ethan, still looking rock-like, managed to produce a smile as he tucked Holly's arm in his, and began to engage the surprised grey-haired couple in a discussion of London's latest musical hit.

Holly, limp with relief now that the need for action was past, found herself leaning against his solid body and enjoying a feeling of security, comfort and . . . a sensation she'd felt once before and discovered she liked very much.

Ethan remained close to her for some time, but she couldn't tell if he was angry or indifferent. Eventually, when his bank manager claimed his attention, he moved away.

For Holly, the next half-hour passed in a sort of glittering haze in which shadowy figures in dark suits and pretty dresses seemed to drift in and out of her vision. Vaguely she was also aware of smiling, talking, checking on empty glasses and trays of food, and doing all the things expected of a hostess. Now and then she noticed Ethan watching her with a kind of perplexity, and sometimes — particularly when she was laughing with one of the male guests — a familiar scowl. It was as if he didn't quite know what to make of her but intended to find out in due time.

His look excited her in unexpected ways, filled her with a singular warmth and anticipation. Yet she had no real idea of what she was expecting.

Then a tall man with glossy black hair and a wide smile took her arm, and drew her behind a table supporting a huge bowl of chrysanthemums and daisies.

'I've been watching you,' he explained. 'You seem to be a remarkably capable young woman.'

'I do?' Holly eyed him warily, remembering Hands. 'Er — thank you.'

He inclined his head. 'Yes, indeed. Capable, and decorative as well.' He beamed at her, and she was surprised at the unusual whiteness of his teeth.

'Decorative?' she repeated, not quite believing him. No one had ever called her decorative before. 'It's kind of you to say so, but — '

He held up his hand. 'No, don't deny it. I'm sure you're modest as well as becoming.'

As Holly stood gaping at him, not sure how to respond, he suddenly snapped off the head of a yellow daisy and tucked it into her hair.

'What are you doing?' she exclaimed,

in spite of herself amused by his cheerful effrontery. 'I spent ages with the florist choosing those flowers, and — '

'And what better use could they be put to than adorning your beautiful hair?'

'My beautiful . . . ?' Holly choked, sputtered, and finally burst out laughing. This man had a line long enough to reach to the moon, but he was so engaging about it that she couldn't get seriously annoyed. Not when he was patting her on the shoulder and joining in her laughter himself.

They were still laughing when a bulky shadow fell across them, and Holly looked up to see Ethan standing over her.

His smile was humourless, his eyes forbidding, and just for a moment she felt like a schoolgirl caught passing notes.

'I'm glad to see you're enjoying yourself,' he said coldly. 'Hello, Domingo, I hope you won't mind if I cut in.

There are one or two people I want Ms Adams to talk to.'

Holly blinked. He made it sound as though she had fallen down in her duty as a hostess. He was also being extremely rude.

Smiling frozenly, she resisted an impulse to stamp on his feet, and threw an apologetic look at the man he had addressed as Domingo. 'Please excuse me,' she said. 'It's been a pleasure . . . '

'I'll bet,' muttered Ethan, as he hustled her away. 'And what particular pleasure did you have in mind?'

She was conscious of the hardness of his body as he strode beside her, and where his hand gripped her elbow she felt heat. 'Not the pleasure of your company,' she replied tartly, pushing from her mind all thought of pleasures of a very different kind, which she had never experienced or even thought much about up to now.

Ethan didn't answer. Instead he marched her up to a group of chattering matrons, smiled imperiously,

and said, 'My dear, I'd like to introduce you to our top sales people. This is . . . '
He proceeded to reel off a list of names, and as Holly murmured polite greetings and contemplated homicide she couldn't help being impressed by his familiarity with Smart and Yorke's personnel. They came from all over the country, and it wasn't every man in his position who would take the trouble to learn the names of workers he saw only once or twice a year.

She was not impressed, though, when he threw her a repressive look and murmured into her ear that, if it wasn't too much trouble, perhaps she might like to consider entertaining some of the female guests for a change. 'And take that damn flower off,' he growled.

Before Holly could think of a reply, the pixie-faced girl had come up to reclaim his arm.

She turned back to the matrons, all of whom were singing Ethan's praises, and for the rest of the evening her emotions hovered between pride that the reception was going so well, and rage at her unappreciative boss — who, she noticed, was keeping a stern eye on her every move from whatever part of the room he happened to be in. It was as if he was practically daring her to let him down.

It wasn't until Ethan was helping her on with her coat after bidding the last guest farewell that Holly was finally able to ask him what he meant by treating her like a badly behaved schoolgirl.

'Schoolgirl? Hell,' he exclaimed. 'It wasn't any schoolgirl I saw in action this evening.

'In action?' said Holly sweetly. 'I hope you're not trying to say that I encouraged that revolting creature with the hands.'

His fingers tightened on her shoulders. 'No, of course not. I was thinking of your other conquests. You've had quite a successful evening, haven't you, my dear?'

His voice positively purred with

innuendo, and Holly spun round and said furiously, 'Yes, I have. The evening was altogether successful. And if you had any sense of decency you'd thank me, instead of making ridiculous insinuations about my conquests. I did a damn good job for you, Ethan Yorke.'

He frowned, and the grooves between his eyes made him look less sure of himself, less coldly patronising. 'Yes, you did,' he agreed. 'And I do thank you.'

Well, that was better. 'Then what's all this rubbish about conquests?' Holly snapped.

Ethan brushed a hand across his forehead. 'I don't know. You tell me,' he said shortly.

'There's nothing to tell. And why should you care if there was?'

'Hmm.' He shrugged. 'You're right, I shouldn't. I don't. Although I have to admit our friend with the hands got my goat.'

Holly sighed. She didn't know what was the matter with Ethan, other than his usual perversity. But whatever he had done to Hands had done the trick — and for that, at least, she was grateful.

'He got my goat too,' she agreed, pulling a tissue out of her pocket, beginning to blow her nose, then changing her mind. 'What did you do to him? You got rid of him with very little fuss.'

'Easy.' He draped himself against the peach-coloured wall. 'I bent his thumb backwards — slowly. When it reached the point of no return, I imagine he decided retreat was the better part of lechery.'

'Oh.' Holly bit her lip, determined not to laugh. 'Thank you. Was his business very important to you?'

'Not nearly as important as the peace of mind — and body — of my only assistant. You didn't seem to be coping very well.'

'I wasn't,' said Holly, her gaze riveted uncomfortably on the floor. 'I'm not . . . nobody's ever . . . '

'Nobody?' She could tell from the tone of his voice that he didn't believe her.

She shook her head. 'No. Never.'

'Well, I'll be damned.' He put his thumb beneath her chin and tilted her face up. Then, after studying it for a long, tense moment, all at once he grasped the lapels of her coat and began to tug her very slowly towards him. Inexplicably, Holly felt dizzy, and when Ethan's fingers brushed up against her neck she found herself clutching on to him for support.

'Tired?' he asked softly.

She nodded and cast a doubtful glance at his face. He was smiling now — a twisted, enigmatic sort of smile that had a startling effect on her pulse-rate.

She smiled back, feeling shy, as she had never been with him, and an odd look came into his eyes, as if he'd just had a revelation he didn't like.

'What is it?' asked Holly. 'Is something wrong?'

'Maybe,' he answered cryptically.

Quite suddenly Ethan's strange attitude, and the feelings that had disturbed her all evening, caused something inside Holly to flame into a seething desire to force him to abandon his unshakeable control.

'Then you'd better find out, hadn't you?' she taunted him. 'Instead of standing there holding up a perfectly well-constructed wall.'

Ethan's eyes narrowed, and he flexed his shoulders so that the muscles bulged seductively against the dark fabric of his suit.

'I do believe you're right,' he said softly. 'Come here.'

There was something silky and almost threatening about his voice. It made her shiver at the same time as it started a slow burning in her blood. But because she didn't trust the look in his eyes, she backed away.

It proved to be the wrong thing to do. He moved, so swiftly that she didn't see him coming, and in an instant his hands were gripping her upper arms.

She gasped. His closeness, the mysterious glitter in his eyes and a sense that something totally unforeseen was about to happen made her catch her breath and try to break away. But immediately he pushed his hand beneath her hair and curved it round the back of her neck.

'No,' he said. 'Keep still.'

'Ethan,' she managed to choke, 'you can't . . . '

'I can,' he murmured.

Before she could speak, he had bent his head and closed her parted lips with a kiss.

She had always, in a disinterested sort of way, realised that his mouth was sensual and alluring, and she had seen the way women's eyes followed him whenever he crossed a room. But nothing had prepared her for the way her body reacted the moment his lips covered hers. A wave of unbelievable warmth swept through her and turned her limbs limp with a formless longing. Her head spun, and the world as she had known it turned upside-down. Without even being aware of what she was doing, she put her arms round Ethan's neck to pull him closer — and in a moment she felt his hands inside her coat, on her waist, and the lean, hard length of his frame was pressed against her own yielding softness.

His kiss was gentle at first, exploratory, but soon it became firmer, more purposeful, and as she ran her hands across his back his velvet tongue slipped in between her lips to taste the welcoming sweetness deep within.

Very vaguely, in what was left of her mind, Holly knew that this kiss could not go on forever. But she wanted it to. She felt as if every minute of her life had been leading up to this one incredible moment. Suddenly the man who had exasperated her, bossed her around, and frequently driven her to distraction over the last four months had become the sun at the centre of her universe. She could no longer distinguish magic from reality.

But Ethan could, for after a while he removed her arms from his neck and held her away.

She staggered, and he backed her up against the wall. Very gradually the room swam into focus again. 'Ethan,' she murmured, because he was all she could think of. 'Ethan . . . '

'Yes?' he said, politely, as if she'd asked him a question.

'Ethan, I . . . what . . . what happened?'

'I kissed you,' he said, casually straightening his tie. 'And you kissed me back. Rather satisfactorily, I might add. You surprised me.'

'Oh. Did I? I . . . I'm glad it was . . . satisfactory.'

A corner of his mouth slanted up. 'Are you? But of course you always aim to please, don't you, Holly? Even when you disapprove of the person you're pleasing.'

'I don't disapprove of you. Not any more.'

'Good. Obviously I should have

kissed you sooner. I'm afraid it just didn't occur to me.'

'No,' said Holly. 'I know it didn't, because it didn't occur to me either.' She frowned, not knowing what to make of the fact that he seemed so cool and uninvolved. 'But now that you have . . . '

'Yes? Now that I have . . . ?

His eyebrows arched up in that way that always confused her, and she forgot what she meant to say, and said instead, 'What happens next, Ethan?' When he put his hands in his pockets and didn't answer, she added hurriedly, 'I mean, where do you and I go from here?'

'Go? I wasn't aware . . . ' He stopped, then started again. 'Well, I suppose we could always go to bed. But office romances never work, do they? And I'm not sure I want to lose a good assistant.'

6

'Oh!' Holly gasped. 'I didn't mean . . . I don't want . . . '

'No, I was afraid you didn't,' said Ethan, with just the barest hint of a smile.

Holly gaped at him. Was this cool, provoking stranger the man who had just swept her off her practical feet? She closed her eyes, struggling to gather her shattered wits. Yes, of course he was. And in a way he still resembled the autocratic, disciplined man she worked for — the man who sneered at office liaisons and, when it suited him, amused himself with beauties like Diane.

'Was that why you kissed me?' she asked, trying to keep the hurt from her voice.

'Was what why I kissed you? And, incidentally, you did kiss me back.'

'I know.' Holly raised her head and forced herself to look him in the eye. She still felt giddy and disorientated, but she had to know what had been in his mind. 'I mean did you kiss me because I suddenly struck you as a likely candidate for bed? Or . . . or for some other reason?'

'Some other reason. If you must know, I hired you in the first place precisely because bed *didn't* come to mind.'

Holly wondered why his words hit her like a slap in the face. She had wanted honesty. She ought to be grateful that she had got it. 'Oh,' she said, not knowing that her eyes, behind the green glasses, looked as wistful as an injured puppy's. 'I think I guessed that, but . . . '

'But I've moved the goal-posts on you, and now you want to know where you stand.' He sounded resigned, and yet in some way baffled — as if he wasn't sure of the goal-posts himself.

'Yes.' She took a deep breath. She

didn't know how to flirt and play sex games, any more than she'd known how to cope with Hands. But she'd always found that telling the truth worked best. 'I liked you kissing me. Nobody ever has before. But, as I said, I . . . I need to know where we go from here.'

'Holly . . . ' Ethan took a step towards her, held out his hand, and for a moment she thought he meant to take her in his arms. Then a look that might have been frustration — or just plain irritation — flashed across his face, before he turned his back on her abruptly and pounded his forehead with his fist. 'Holly, we don't go anywhere. I admit I shouldn't have kissed you. But you seemed different tonight, and when I saw that randy jackass pawing at you . . . '

'You thought you'd find out if I was worth it,' Holly finished bleakly.

He swung round, eyes dark and unreadable. 'Is that what you think? No, as a matter of fact I discovered I wanted to break a lot more than his thumb — not take over from him. Then I saw you with Domingo, and I forgot you were my sane and sensible assistant. I wanted to kiss you. So I did. But I'd no idea — '

'That I'd think it meant anything,' said Holly with a brittle little laugh. 'Oh, don't worry. I didn't.'

'Holly, don't lie to me. I was going to say I didn't believe you'd never been kissed before. You haven't, have you? If I'd known — '

'If you'd known, you wouldn't have done it, and I'd never have had the thrill of a lifetime,' said Holly, sarcasm dripping from each word.

Ethan drew in his breath and counted very deliberately to ten. 'Oh, yes, I certainly would have done it,' he replied grimly. 'But I'd have made a point of making it memorable. For both of us. Now . . . ' He paused, and then carried on in a different, no-nonsense tone of voice, 'To answer your question, and, since you assure me it meant nothing, I suggest we carry on as we were. You can go back to wearing shapeless suits, I can forget they conceal a surprisingly voluptuous body, and both of us will forget about what happened this evening.' He gave her a practised smile. 'It went very well, by the way. You did an excellent job. Exactly what I hired you to do. Keep it up, and we shouldn't have any further problems.' He took her arm and glanced towards the doorway. 'Come along, I believe I see the vacuum crew approaching.'

'Good,' said Holly. 'And don't worry. I won't have any trouble forgetting.'

His only response was a word she hadn't heard before, and was pretty sure she didn't want to hear again.

In a daze that was part blind fury, part hurt pride, and part a crushing sense of loss, Holly allowed him to lead her down the hall. She was conscious of his hand on her arm, of his firm thigh pressing against her hip, and of the spicy scent of man that was uniquely Ethan's.

What had happened back there in the deserted reception-room amid the empty glasses and the spilled crumbs on the dove-grey carpet? On the surface, the answer to that one was easy. For the first time in her life, a man had kissed her. Really kissed her. Not like Andy's experimental fumblings. And that man was walking beside her. But he had only done it on an impulse because she looked different tonight, and she had challenged his masculine complacence. It didn't mean anything to him, and he hadn't expected it to mean anything to her. Asking him what would happen next had been the height of childish stupidity. What a naïve little fool he must think her.

Frowning, and wondering why she felt as if he'd kicked her instead of kissed her, Holly stole a glance at his face. It was empty; there was nothing there except a brisk determination to get her home and get the evening over. And on Monday he would expect her to appear in the office and carry on as if nothing had happened. Of course, from his point of view, nothing had — except that she had dented his ego a little by telling him his kiss was forgettable.

Ethan helped her into the Maserati with his usual attentive urbanity, and took off smartly down the street. In no time at all they were back in Chiswick.

Holly didn't realise she was holding her breath until he took her hand at the door, said, 'Thank you, Ms Adams,' very formally, and swung back down the path to the gate. She exhaled very slowly as unexpected tears stung her eyes.

* * *

Holly spent most of Sunday sitting on her bench in the park as she tried to sort out her feelings, and decide what course, if any, she ought to take.

The feeling part wasn't too difficult. Ethan had awakened her in ways that were totally new to her. He had opened a door for her, only to slam it in her face. It wasn't that she was in love with him, but . . . was it possible she *could* love him? If only he would let her? But of course he wouldn't. She was a fool even to think it.

Ethan wanted an assistant in his office, not a lover. The question now was whether she could continue to fill that position.

When Monday morning followed a sleepless night, she was still no closer to an answer.

But by halfway through the day she was.

Ethan had glanced at his watch the moment she walked into his office. She was still hurt and angry with him, but one look at the cool slant of his mouth made her feel as shy and awkward as any fifteen-year-old gazing on the hero of her dreams. Then, when his first words were, 'Ah, Ms Adams, you're five minutes late,' awkwardness turned into frozen indignation.

She paused with her hand on the doorknob. It was the first time she'd been late since she started working for him, and she stayed at least ten minutes after hours every evening — as well he knew. 'I'm sorry,' she said woodenly, her gaze on the silver pen gripped too tightly between his square-tipped fingers. 'There was a power failure on the train.'

'That's no excuse. You should have left home earlier.'

'I did,' said Holly, with icicles dripping from her voice. 'We were stuck in the tunnel for an hour.'

'Well, don't let it happen again,' he replied with baffling male logic, and dropped his gaze a little too obviously to the print-out on the desk in front of him.

Holly glared at the rich brown of his hair, and thought how much she would like to pull it . . . and run her fingers through the thickly curling waves . . . then slowly, very slowly, down his spine . . .

She swallowed and pulled herself up with a gasp just as Ethan looked up from the print-out.

Their eyes met, and for a second she thought she saw a reflection of her own formless hunger, a brief softening, before he frowned and said curtly, 'That will be all, thank you, Holly.'

She eyed the paperweight on his desk with longing, but remembered in time that she wasn't fond of cleaning up blood.

Fifteen minutes later, as she was booting up her computer, Ethan thumped a half-full mug of coffee on her desk.

'This is much too weak,' he rasped. 'You'd better brew another pot, Adams.'

'It's the same brew I always make,' said Holly. 'And, if you don't mind, it's *Ms* Adams to you.'

'I do mind. And I still want a fresh cup of coffee.'

'Over your head?' asked Holly, smiling demurely.

'Adams, I warn you — '

'And I warn *you*, Mr Yorke, that if you're planning to keep this up you'd better start looking for a new assistant.'

She turned back to her keyboard, but Ethan caught her wrist before she could punch in a word.

'I'm thinking about it,' he said shortly. 'If I were you, I wouldn't push your luck.'

She glanced pointedly at the hand circling her arm and tried not to think about the fiery needles it was sending through her veins. Ethan followed her gaze, and released her so suddenly that her knuckles hit the edge of the desk.

'Ouch,' she said.

He was already turning away, but at once he paused and said, 'Holly? Did I hurt you?' The words were abrupt, but there was genuine concern in his eyes.

'No,' said Holly. 'Better luck next time.'

Ethan made a sound that might have been a laugh but was probably an explosion, and strode back into his office and closed the door.

'Well done,' muttered Holly at his departing back. 'You *would* manage not to slam it.'

The phone rang, and she picked it up and said, 'Yes?' so sharply that she felt obliged to explain. 'Sorry. I'm having a rather difficult morning.'

'Translate difficult boss,' said an amused voice on the other end of the line. 'Could this be my lucky chance?'

Holly frowned. There was something vaguely familiar about that voice, but he wasn't a regular caller . . .

'David Domingo. Hall and Goodman. I met you at Saturday's reception.'

Of course. The man with the glossy black hair and the wide smile who had put the flower behind her ear.

Holly relaxed against the back of the chair. After Ethan's bad temper and badgering, her ego could do with more of that kind of stroking. And if she remembered correctly, David Domingo was the general manager of Smart and Yorke's closest rival in the clothing business. The two firms maintained wary business ties, mainly to keep an eye on each other's products.

'Yes, of course, Mr Domingo,' she

said pleasantly. 'What can I do for you?'

'As a matter of fact, I'm hoping we can do something for each other. Margaret Yeoman, the head of our public relations department, has been forced to resign unexpectedly. Heart trouble.'

'I'm sorry,' said Holly, mystified. 'But — '

David Domingo chuckled. 'But you don't see what it has to do with you. The point is, Ms Adams, I was very impressed with your performance on Saturday night. You combined unobtrusive elegance and style with minute attention to the needs of your guests. I understand it was your expertise that ensured the evening went without a hitch.'

'Mine?' said Holly, trying not to squeak. As far as she was concerned, Hands was a definite hitch, and after that she had floated through most of the evening in blissful unawareness of her guests.

'Yes, indeed. That's why I have a

proposition to put before you.'

'Really?' She decided not to jump to the obvious — and improbable — conclusion.

'Really. I'd like to talk to you — about the possibility of your taking on Margaret's job. Will you have lunch with me today, Ms Adams?'

Holly took the phone away from her ear and stared doubtfully into the receiver. It didn't *seem* to be defective.

'I don't know — ' she began.

'I'm offering double whatever you're making now,' he added encouragingly.

'But . . . ' No, it didn't make sense. How could David Domingo possibly know he wanted her for the job on the basis of one night's extremely brief acquaintance? Why he hardly knew her, and —

'Lunch, Ms Adams? I'll send my chauffeur to pick you up. Will one o'clock suit you?'

His chauffeur . . . But of course he *wouldn't* care to be seen absconding with Ethan's personal assistant, thought

Holly wryly. On the other hand, would she care to have lunch with a man she'd only met once, in order to discuss a job she didn't want?

'Adams, what the hell . . . ?' Ethan's roar penetrated the wall. Holly sighed. He must have discovered something else to find fault with.

'Yes, one o'clock will be fine,' she said quickly. 'I'll look forward to it.'

'Excellent.' He hung up the phone, and Holly, with another sigh, went to see what had aroused her boss's ire.

'You're shouting,' she said coldly. 'In case you've forgotten, I'm not Ellen.'

Ethan flung down his pen and stood up. 'I'm well aware that you're not my sister, thank you,' he snapped, slapping his palms on to the desk as if he'd like to be slapping them on her. 'You're my assistant, and I'd like to know what in hell you've done with the Benzoni file.'

'Isn't that it there?' asked Holly, managing not to raise her voice and pointing to a thick folder on the filing-cabinet beside his desk.

Ethan picked it up, glared at it, and slammed it down in front of her. 'All right. I thought I told you to go on wearing sensible suits. That . . . that blue thing shows far too much leg.'

'Mr Yorke,' said Holly, at her most formal, and drawing herself up to her full, unimpressive height, 'the fact that you decided to kiss me on Saturday night does not give you the right to dictate what I wear. And this 'blue thing', as you call it, is a dress.'

'Is it indeed?' To her consternation, instead of growling the angry retort she expected, he gave her a smile that reminded her of a wolf in pursuit of a light snack, and began to rake his eyes very deliberately from her face down to her ankles, then back up again. For all her resentment, she felt a flare of heat deep in her abdomen. When he came to her breasts, which suddenly seemed to be pressing against the soft blue bodice of her dress, he paused and then drawled pensively, 'OK, if you say so, it's a dress. But if you choose to flaunt it around my office, there's a very good chance it will come off — and you'll cease to be my assistant.'

Holly swallowed hard. There was no mistaking the innuendo, and it was so unlike Ethan to behave like an executive Romeo that she found herself blurting indignantly, and with none of the control she wanted to maintain, 'You promised not to request services beyond the call of duty.'

'So I did,' he said softly, and Holly swallowed again, mesmerised by the tough outline of his body in a dark grey power suit, as he stood with his legs a little apart and his arms crossed, exuding an almost tangible aura of raw and blatant virility. 'So I did. How very shortsighted of me.'

Holly swallowed again, and stepped backwards, and all at once his amused and speculative expression vanished, and he said roughly, 'Oh, for heaven's sake get out of here, Ms Adams. I'm not going to put you on your back across my desk.'

'I . . . I didn't think you were,' said Holly, closing her mind to the erotic imaginings his turn of phrase evoked. She ran her tongue over her lips, and added with false brightness, 'Is there anything else I can do for you, Mr Yorke?'

'Very possibly,' he muttered. 'I said get out of here, Adams.'

Holly forbore from reminding him that her name wasn't Adams, and got.

But her hopes that she would hear no more from Ethan that morning were very soon summarily dashed.

By the time one o'clock came around she was seriously contemplating locking him in his office and refusing to release him until he was ready to stop behaving like one of the less agreeable inmates of the zoo.

In the space of three hours he had managed to criticise every letter and report she wrote, every word she had spoken, the way she held her pen and answered the phone, and even the new green glasses which on Saturday he had deigned to admire.

'And you're wearing too much make-up,' he'd snapped, when he'd finally run out of ammunition.

Holly ignored him. Obviously he wasn't himself, and if he was going to take exception to pale pink lipstick and a bit of eyeshadow there wasn't any point in arguing with him.

Lunch with a man who admired her ability and didn't treat her as a cross between a doormat and a possible bedmate would come as a blessed relief.

'Holly?' Ethan's voice stopped her just as she was heading for the lift.

She hesitated, then reluctantly turned round.

He was standing with his fists bunched at his thighs and his jaw thrust out as if he were daring her to hit it. But the dark lights burning in his eyes were much less easy to interpret.

'Holly,' he said, as if he were ordering her to take a letter, 'have lunch with me.'

'What?' She gaped at him. After behaving like a sexy bear with a hangover all morning, did he actually think she would allow him to disrupt her lunch hour as well?

'I said have lunch with me,' he repeated.

'I'm afraid I can't,' replied Holly in her frostiest tone. 'I already have a luncheon engagement.'

'Then cancel it.'

'You,' she replied, turning her back on him, 'are without a doubt the most arrogant and overbearing man I've ever met. And I have no intention of cancelling it.'

The lift came then, and she stepped into it without looking back.

But just as the door closed she thought she heard Ethan utter one brief, very explicit word. It was new to her, but its meaning was abundantly clear.

Ten minutes later she subsided on to the seat of David Domingo's chauffeur-driven Rolls, and allowed the richness of the interior to enfold her in a soothing cocoon.

She felt battered and exhausted, both mentally and physically, and she was grateful for the time to recoup herself in private. Later she would think about what she was going to do about Ethan, but for now all she could do was breathe deeply and stare at the passing stream of traffic. She was also grateful that David had chosen the quiet, sober elegance of his club for this meeting, rather than a trendy modern hotel.

After one look at her face he ordered a very good brandy. Later, with gentle authority, he ordered a light but superbly cooked meal. Holly smiled her appreciation.

It was a relief not to have to think for herself for a while.

By the time they had finished eating, she felt more relaxed and at ease than she had in weeks. David had a certain charm, which he knew how to use, and it was good to be told she was smart, intelligent and just the woman he wanted for the job. She no longer felt his offer needed to make much sense, and loyalty to Ethan began to seem like misguided quixotry. Ethan was entirely capable of looking after himself, and after his behaviour this morning he had no right to expect her allegiance.

Just the same, some residue of conscience — or was it something that had nothing to do with conscience, and everything to do with the memory of a kiss? — made her ask David if he would mind waiting until the next day for her decision.

'Of course not,' he said, black eyes twinkling at her. 'I know you won't disappoint me.'

If he knew that, it was more than she knew herself, she thought despairingly as she reclined against the upholstery in the Rolls. David's offer was very attractive — in fact he wasn't unattractive himself — but if she left Smart and Yorke she wouldn't see Ethan any more. And although she knew she ought to consider that a bonus, for some reason the prospect of a future without Ethan in it seemed very bleak.

After a while, she was forced to acknowledge that the reason was a kiss.

Oh, God! She *couldn't* be falling . . .

Stop it, Holly, she told herself disgustedly. That kiss was an aberration. He didn't mean it to happen, and he wishes it hadn't. That's why he's been acting like such a bear. And only a masochist would go on working for him when she can make twice as much money working for somebody else with a better disposition and probably a better job.

She was scowling when she sat down at her desk, and she didn't bother to see if Ethan was in.

As it turned out, he wasn't, and the afternoon passed uneventfully until he strode out of the lift just before four o'clock looking like Dracula in search of a victim — a role which Holly suspected he intended her to fill.

'Well? Did you enjoy your lunch?' he asked icily.

'Very much.' She picked up a pencil and began to scribble notes on a pad.

At once she felt his fist close over her hand as he twisted the pencil out of her fingers and threw it down on the desk. 'I'm talking to you,' he said, in a voice that should have made her tremble but made her want to hit him instead. 'Kindly pay attention.'

'Very well,' she replied, conquering the urge to violence and raising her head. 'I'm listening.'

'Good. Because I'd like you to know, Ms Adams, that I don't appreciate disloyalty to the firm.'

'I beg your pardon?' Holly wondered if he was psychic — and hoped she sounded bored and unconcerned.

'Don't play games with me. You had lunch with Domingo, didn't you.'

'Yes, I did. Is that a crime?' When he pressed his fists down on her blotter so hard that she thought they'd go right through it she added tiredly, 'How did you know?'

'I happen to belong to the same club.

The fact that you declined to delight me with your company didn't strike me as any reason to forgo lunch.'

'Oh. I didn't see you.'

'No, you were too busy basking in the light of Domingo's charms.'

'Actually,' said Holly, 'I was basking in the rare pleasure of being entertained by a man who didn't treat me as if I'm some kind of doormat. In fact I enjoyed it so much that I'm afraid you'll have to find somewhere else to wipe your feet.'

'What's that supposed to mean?' He bent over until his chin was almost touching her forehead.

'It means . . . ' She gulped, trying to dislodge the sudden lump in her throat. 'It means I'm resigning. Mr Domingo has offered me a job.'

Ethan drew a sharp breath, and then let it out so forcefully that it fanned her hair. 'Has he, now?' he murmured. 'With fringe benefits too, I imagine.'

Holly gasped. Was he suggesting . . . ? No, surely not. Men had never suggested that sort of thing about her.

Although since she'd changed her image and her attitude, maybe . . .

'Yes,' she said coolly. 'With benefits.'

'And what did you offer him in return?' He was looking at her as if he suspected she'd offered David her soul, along with something more tangible.

'My best effort to do a good job for him,' she replied, as if it were the only possible answer — and as if she didn't feel like wrapping her arms around the difficult man scowling down at her, and pulling his glorious lips over hers. For one insane moment, she had a sense that he felt the same need, but all he said was,

'I see.'

Holly frowned and started to stand. There was something in his eyes now that unnerved her, something barren and empty that made him appear more like a robot than flesh and blood. Suddenly she had to get away.

'Where do you think you're going?' He caught her arm as she tried to make a bolt for the lift.

'To . . . to powder my nose.'

'No, you're not. I like it shiny.'

'What?' Holly looked up at him, bewildered by the startling change in his voice. It was no longer hard and threatening, but deep and warm, playing with her nerve-ends like the strings of a guitar.

'I said I like it shiny. Holly, I won't let you leave just to pay me back for behaving like a jerk. I don't want you to work for Domingo. I want you here.'

She felt fire where his hand touched her skin, and his words were like unbreakable strands of silk, binding her to him until she didn't even want to escape. But how could she stay with a man who was as unpredictable as Ethan had become — one minute acting like Genghis Khan, the next like Chaucer's 'verray, parfit gentil knyght'? She could cope, perhaps, if things were different. If she didn't . . . She shied away from the thought. Anyway, things weren't different. They never would be.

'You . . . you are a jerk,' she said

shakily. 'But I'm not leaving just to pay you back.'

'Then why? Money?'

'There's nothing wrong with wanting to earn more money,' she said, stung by the implied accusation. 'But it's not that.'

'No?' Ethan's voice was deep and carefully controlled. 'It's the fact that I kissed you and then treated you like a doormat, isn't it?' He raked a hand through his hair, and for a moment she saw a gentleness in his eyes, which turned swiftly to resignation. 'All right, Holly. I'm not going to grovel, but I do apologise. And I do want you to stay. So I'll try not to wipe my feet on you more than usual, promise not to kiss you again, and if you want more money it's yours. How's that for a magnanimous offer?'

'Not good enough.' Holly turned her back on him so he wouldn't see the hurt she was sure must be written in her eyes. Didn't he know that she *wanted* him to kiss her again? He must know. And he was pretending he didn't want to because he wanted to keep her in his office as an efficient but undistracting cog in the corporate machine.

'I see.' His warm breath teased the ends of her hair. 'Then what must I do to sweeten the pot?'

'Nothing,' she muttered. 'There's nothing you can do, Ethan.' And there wasn't, because she knew now that she wouldn't be able to work close to him every day without ever giving away what was in her heart. It wasn't love, of course, but she wanted so desperately to touch him, to hold him in her arms as she had before . . . No, it would be as much as she could do to carry on until he hired someone else.

But his hands were on her shoulders now, firm and hard, and she could feel the length of his lean body against her back.

'OK,' he said harshly. 'In that case the deal's off. I'll go back to being a jerk, shall I?'

Before Holly had a chance to ask what he meant, he had spun her around. For a split second his hands lingered close to her neck, and she saw frustration — or was it just cynicism? — in his eyes. She thought — hoped? — he meant to kiss her. Then the hunger, if that was what it was, faded and he dropped his arms and stepped back.

Holly stared at a dark speck on the carpet. When she found the courage to raise her head, she saw that Ethan was looking at her almost as if he'd never seen her before and was wondering what she was doing in her own office. 'When do you plan to desert me?' he asked, as if her answer were of no great importance.

'I . . . as soon as you can find someone else.' Holly spoke quietly. 'I don't want my leaving to cause you any inconvenience.'

'Neither do I,' he agreed. 'However, it's not the first time it's happened. I believe I'll survive.'

Holly wasn't worrying about his survival. At this moment all she could think about was her own. She couldn't even put her mind to his odd remark that it had happened before. What had happened? Did he mean some earlier assistant had left him for pastures greener? She shrugged. It didn't matter. A week from now she might not even be working for Ethan any more. Strange how that thought made her feel cold.

But a week later Ethan seemed no nearer to finding a replacement, and in spite of his now distant and strictly businesslike attitude towards her Holly found herself increasingly reluctant to leave. Sometimes, when he didn't know she was watching him, she caught again that look of angry frustration in his eyes, and then his lips would twist in the cynical curve she so disliked and he would go off and slam something — usually his fist on a desk. At those times Holly always felt like crying.

In the end, after another week had passed, during which Ethan continued to refuse all the hopeful applicants for her job, Holly knew she could stand it no longer. She didn't want to leave, but if she was to maintain her grip on her sanity she had no choice.

First thing on a Tuesday morning she marched into his office, took the report he was reading out of his hands, and said, 'Right. Mr Yorke, you will either choose one of the three applicants Miss Lovejoy has scheduled for today, or you will find yourself without an assistant. You have so far turned down four very well-qualified ladies because they tint their hair, three more because their finger-nails are too long, and seven because you say they're too eager to please. The only one you've even vaguely consid-ered is that mousy little Mrs Sneed, and she says she doesn't want the job.'

After two weeks spent enduring Ethan's coldly correct behaviour, which didn't even hint at the warmth and humour that had made working with him bearable in the past, Holly's patience was at an end, and her nerves completely unravelled. 'Now,' she went on, 'we have a Ms Willoughby, a Mrs Singh, and a Miss Duval. Miss Lovejoy hasn't scheduled any more appointments and I don't intend her to. I'm leaving at the end of the week.'

Ethan raised his head, and the look he gave her sizzled with such naked and unexpected sensuality that she found herself reaching blindly for a chair that wasn't there as the muscles in her legs turned to liquid.

But all he said was, 'Can't wait to try your luck with Domingo, I suppose,' and the corner of his mouth curled in a sneer.

'I can't wait to work for someone who smiles occasionally, and . . . ' She stopped. Ethan had parted his lips and was baring his teeth at her in a feral parody of a grin.

'Stop it,' she cried. 'Ethan why are you doing this? You don't want me to stay, and yet you refuse to make it easy for me to leave.'

'Who said I don't want you to stay?

I seem to remember offering you a rise.'

'Yes, but . . . ' Her voice trailed off. Was that why he had become so cold and distant? Because she was leaving him? How stupid of her not to have realised that before. Of course he resented her going to the opposition. Besides, she was a convenience he was loath to give up. And apparently he had never liked David.

For a moment her resolution wavered. She didn't really *want* to leave Ethan. It was just that she found herself wanting more of him than he was willing to give. The fact was, his physical presence had become an agonising aphrodisiac. She couldn't bear being forced to look at him all day and never touch. And it wasn't only that. She felt more than a physical need. If she stayed —

'Well?' said Ethan, interrupting her thoughts.

'Well what?'

'Are you still determined to leave? If it's money — '

'It's not money.'

He ran a weary hand over his forehead. 'It's always money in the end. Never mind. Send in Ms Willoughby. You can leave at the end of the week. Domingo's welcome to you.'

Holly opened her mouth to reply, but he had gone back to reading his report.

She sent in Ms Willoughby, and Ethan hired her on the spot.

On Friday, after Holly had cleaned out her desk, she went in to say goodbye to her ex-boss. He was on the phone.

She hesitated, and he raised his eyebrows at her, propped one foot on the edge of his desk, and lifted a hand in casual farewell as he carried deliberately on with his conversation. From the sensuous murmur of his voice, Holly deduced that he was talking to a woman.

She gave him what she hoped was a smile and not a grimace, and stumbled out of his office. As she made for the lift, she felt tears pricking at her eyes, and she moved faster in case Ethan should take it into his head to come after her. At any moment she half expected to feel the touch of his hand on her arm.

But there was no hand, and when the doors closed behind her she was alone.

★ ★ ★

'Ms Willoughby, what have you done with the Stonehouse file?' Ethan spoke wearily, in the certainty that Ms Willoughby's answer would fail to satisfy.

'I haven't seen it, Mr Yorke. Not since Mr Blackstone in Accounting asked to borrow it.'

He glared at her. 'I thought I told you no file was to go out of this office without my permission.'

'Yes, but — '

Ethan tuned her out. In the month that the lanky and long-nosed Ms Willoughby had been with him, he had heard every excuse known to woman for her continual flouting of his orders. Plausible excuses, every one. Ms Willoughby always acted from the highest motives. And she had been sufficiently good at her job, and sufficiently unobtrusive, to make him disinclined to spend time breaking in another assistant. But this business with the Stonehouse file was the last straw. That file was highly confidential, and if it found its way into unauthorised hands the results could be extremely awkward for Smart and Yorke.

'Ms Willoughby,' he snapped, interrupting the flow of her alibi, 'you're fired. You can pick up your severance cheque from Mr Haslett.'

He strode to the door and slammed it on her indignant face before picking up the phone to call Accounting.

By the time the file was back under lock and key, Ms Willoughby had unleashed a formidable display of dudgeon, and left with her nose in the air. The dudgeon would have been more convincing if she hadn't spoiled it with the triumphant announcement that she had already accepted a better job from Hall and Goodman.

Hall and Goodman, mused Ethan, steepling his fingers beneath his chin, and fixing a dubious eye on the stale remnants left in his coffee-cup. He didn't give a damn where Ms Willoughby intended to spread her brand of mayhem next, but Holly also worked for Hall and Goodman. He tilted his head at the ceiling, and, not for the first time since Holly had left him, he cursed her under his breath for her desertion.

Hell! He was without an assistant again. He needed Holly. She was the best damn assistant he'd ever had, and he wanted her back. He missed her unassuming but businesslike presence in his office, and he missed . . . Well, dammit, he just missed her. And for the life of him he couldn't imagine why he had let her go. He drummed his fingers on the edge of his desk. Oh, he shouldn't have kissed her, of course.

That had been a mistake, albeit a surprisingly pleasant one. But as he had no intention of letting it happen again . . .

Yes. He made up his mind and leaned over to pick up the phone. Then he put it down again. There were those rumours to be taken into account . . . Maybe more active measures were called for than could be easily handled over the phone.

He smiled grimly. If things went as planned, Ms Holly Adams was in for a shock.

* * *

Holly smiled across the table at David. It was the fourth time he had taken her for lunch since she joined the firm, and on each occasion he had chosen a popular and highly visible restaurant quite unlike his quiet and dignified club. This one was decorated to look like a landlubber's idea of the interior of an ocean liner, with nets on the walls, colourful fish in tanks, and tablecloths patterned with anchors. Holly sometimes felt that David wanted to be *seen* with her more than he actually wanted to be with her. But he was attentive in a distracted sort of way, and she appreciated the chance to discuss any problems related to her job — which she knew she ought to find challenging and exciting, but somehow didn't. She couldn't seem to care about it in the way she had cared at Smart and Yorke's.

When she allowed herself time to think, which she tried not to, Holly had to admit that she missed Ethan. Terribly. Somehow, in those months she had worked with him, he had managed to become a part of her life. It wasn't that she was in love with him, of course. But sometimes, when she remembered his arrogant smile, his deep voice, and the way he had believed she could do anything she wanted, she felt such a rush of desolation that she wondered if she'd lost something irreplaceable

— something she had never had, and now would never have.

Lately, apart from David, a couple of men at the office had asked her out. They were nice men, but she had turned them down without altogether knowing why. Barbara had called her an idiot, a nincompoop and a numbskull, and been disgusted with her.

'What are you smiling at?' David's question brought Holly back to her surroundings, which included the cold eye of an overfed goldfish.

'At you,' she said quickly. 'It was kind of you to invite me, David.'

He smiled back. 'Maybe I had an ulterior motive.'

'Had you?' She put her head on one side and pulled at the hem of her yellow summer dress. 'What sort of motive?'

'Ah, that's . . . Wait a minute. Speaking of motives . . . ' He broke off and grabbed for her hand across the table. 'My dear Holly . . . ' Incomprehensibly, he was raising his voice and gazing into her eyes with the look of an amorous Pekingese. 'Last night you made me very happy. I was sure you would, but I never dreamed — '

As Holly was struck dumb with her mouth open, a heavy hand gripped her shoulder from behind.

'Keep it up, Domingo, and you'll be doing your dreaming in hospital.' Ethan's voice rang out, cool and clipped, in the sudden silence. 'Holly, you're coming with me.'

7

Holly grabbed the sides of her chair, dazed, but still in command of her senses. 'No, I'm not,' she said. 'I'm having lunch with David.'

'You've finished lunch and you're coming with me.' Ethan spoke evenly, as though there were no question of her non-compliance.

'David . . . ' She looked to her employer for support, even as Ethan put a hand under her arm to pull her up.

But David was concentrating on Ethan, and there was a very strange look on his face. As Holly stared down at him, waiting for him to voice some objection to this high-handed interruption of his lunch, she saw that he was actually smiling. It was a triumphant, exultant smile, as though he had just pulled off a corporate coup.

'Come on, Holly,' said Ethan.

'Don't be ridiculous,' she snapped.

'I'm not being ridiculous. If I'm not mistaken, your friend here has already achieved his objective. Or he thinks he has. Your usefulness to him, my dear, is at an end.'

'What are you talking about?' Holly wished he would take his hand off her arm. It was sending all kinds of unwanted impulses to her brain, and just seeing him again, exuding his brand of dominant sexuality, was suddenly almost more than she could bear.

'He's talking about my wife, Gloria,' said David, his smile now stretched into a grin. 'Tit for tat, Yorke. Your little lady is quite a charmer.'

'Who has just resigned her position with Hall and Goodman,' replied Ethan grimly. 'And another time, Domingo, why don't you try thinking with your head instead of your — '

'Not in front of Holly, please,' David broke in with a frown.

Holly looked from one hostile face to the other, and decided she had had more than enough of both men. They seemed to be engaged in some private feud in which she was an unwilling pawn. And she wasn't putting up with it any longer. Besides, neither one of them was really interested in her.

She twisted her arm out of Ethan's grasp, picked up her bag, and threaded her way through the tables of open-mouthed diners as if she were being pursued by the model shark hanging over the bar.

It wasn't until she found herself running down Piccadilly with no particular idea of where she was heading that it occurred to her she had nowhere to go. Ethan had resigned her job for her, which in itself wouldn't matter. But the fact that David had made no attempt to detain her might make a difference. It could be true that he didn't need her in his office any more — that some mysterious purpose of his own had been achieved.

The feeling that she was a pawn in an irritating masculine power struggle became stronger, and along with the feeling came anger.

How dared Ethan barge in and mess up her life as if he owned her, just as she was at last finding her feet in the executive job market?

'Ethan Yorke, if I could just get my hands on you at this moment . . . ' she muttered, to the amazement of a passing gaggle of tourists.

'Sounds promising. Here's your opportunity.' Ethan brushed past and stopped right in front of her with a hard little smile on his lips.

'Please get out of my way,' said Holly, successfully conquering her first idiotic instinct, which was to take up his challenge and throw her arms around him.

'Why? Do you have somewhere special to go?'

As this comment so closely echoed her thoughts of a few seconds earlier, Holly found herself clenching her fists to stop herself from entertaining the crowds with an expert demonstration of eye scratching. Not that she *was* an expert, she thought gloomily, but she could use the practice.

'No,' she said coldly. 'Thanks to you, I *don't* have anywhere to go.'

'Oh, I imagine Domingo will keep you on if you insist,' he said offhandedly. 'He thinks his object has been accomplished, but he's bright enough to recognise a hot property when he sees one. However, I'm hoping you'll come to see things my way.'

'What do you mean by that?' asked Holly, digging her nails into her palms.

'I'll explain when we're somewhere less public.' He glanced up at the warm teal-blue of the sky. 'I think we can safely assume it won't rain. Shall we find a secluded bench in the park, or would you prefer to come back to my flat?'

'I'd prefer to go home,' said Holly. 'Goodbye, Ethan.' She spun round and started to walk briskly in the direction of Green Park station. But when she realised Ethan was right behind her, and that at any moment he was likely to grab her, she veered to the right and hurried down a side-street which she hoped would eventually lead her into Bond Street. She could always catch the Tube from there.

So intent was she on getting away from him that she didn't realise a white Maserati had pulled up beside her until a door opened, and hard fingers closed around her wrist.

The next moment she was sprawled in the passenger seat, the door was pulled firmly shut behind her, and the car was purring rapidly down the street.

'Hey,' she cried. 'Ethan, you can't — '

'I can. I have.'

She sat up and reached for the seatbelt, making a supreme effort to get a grip on herself. There was no sense in arguing with a brick wall, but this was ridiculous. Why had Ethan, controlled and decisive master of a business empire, suddenly turned into a pirate of the old-fashioned kind? Perhaps in her girlish fantasies she had once thought it might be romantic to be kidnapped. The reality was decidedly different. But the car was moving fast, as it invariably did in Ethan's masterful hands, and there was no way she would be able to escape until he stopped.

'Where are you taking me?' she asked frigidly.

'To my flat. It's not far. I'm afraid the park is out of the question now, since some form of restraint seems in order.'

'Are you planning to tie me up, then?' Holly jeered.

'Only if it's necessary.'

He spoke so calmly that Holly began to wonder if he meant it. She stopped glaring out of the window and stole a glance at his face. But it was forbiddingly blank, and told her nothing. For the first time since he'd hijacked her, Holly began to feel a little afraid. After all, how well did she really know Ethan? He seemed normal, if a trifle reserved. But he wasn't used to being thwarted, and she wasn't sure how he might react if she tried to escape from him again.

When he smiled — a white, mocking smile — and patted her carelessly on the knee, she had a sudden disturbing feeling he had read her thoughts.

Seconds later he pulled up a narrow street off Park Lane, and before she could even think of making a run for it he had her door open and was escorting her through an arched doorway and into a lift.

It opened directly into a bright and spacious apartment overlooking Hyde Park. Somehow Holly had expected Ethan's furnishings would be of the practical and coldly modern kind. But she was wrong. He favoured muted colours, certainly — off-white walls and restful pale green fabrics — but two walls were wholly taken up with a colourful assortment of books, and the few pictures he had on display were anything but modern. Holly didn't know much about paintings, but when she recognised the signatures she almost let out a whistle.

'You're impressed,' said Ethan, observing her wide-eyed astonishment. 'Did you imagine I lived in a dungeon?'

'It would have been appropriate,' muttered Holly.

'Cheer up. I keep the rack and the cat-o'-nine-tails in the bedroom.' He draped himself against a bookcase and nodded at a soft green love-seat. 'Sit down.'

'For the inquisition?' enquired Holly derisively.

'If you insist. I aim to please.'

With as much dignity as she could muster, she stepped past him and sat down on the edge of the seat. 'Are you going to explain the point of this charade?' she demanded, when he didn't speak.

'Charade?' He smiled lazily and rested his head on a leather-bound volume of Tennyson.

Just his speed, thought Holly. 'Theirs not to reason why . . . ' Personally she favoured Dylan Thomas and the more modern poets. 'Well? What else could you call it?' she snapped.

'I imagine your friend, Domingo, would call it retribution or revenge.'

Holly frowned. His voice was dry as the desert, and as usual his expression gave nothing away. But he looked very much in charge of his world, lounging there in his grey pin-stripe with his jacket open and his arms loosely crossed on his chest. Just as long as he didn't think he was in charge of her . . . She glanced round the room, seeking some means of strategic retreat.

'There's the fire-escape,' observed Ethan, correctly interpreting her look. 'But I wouldn't advise it. I tried it once and had a tub of water poured over me for my pains.'

'Really?' She tried to sound uninterested but failed. 'How come?'

'The lady was fresh out of boiling oil. I expect water was the next best thing.'

Holly felt a certain sympathy for the unknown lady, but she couldn't quite manage to suppress a grin. 'You're not making sense,' she told him. 'Why should you be breaking into your own apartment?'

'I wasn't. I was breaking out of it.'

'But why?'

He shrugged. 'Would you believe I honestly don't remember? I was very young, very foolish and very drunk. The lady, I suspect, was not amused. In any case, I wouldn't recommend the fire-escape if you're thinking of staging a break-out.'

He was smiling now, but with such maddening complacency that Holly found herself giving him the sort of look she usually reserved for the lesser invertebrates.

The glitter in his eye became sharper. 'I think I have a solution to your problem,' he murmured, smoothing a hand over his jaw.

'What problem?' she asked suspiciously.

'The problem of your being unemployed.'

'Oh.' Holly thought about that. For just a moment she had forgotten what had brought her to this pass. 'Ethan, I wasn't unemployed until you barged into that restaurant. And David hasn't given me the sack . . . ' She hesitated, but curiosity won out over her desire to launch into a pointed harangue on the subject of his manners, ethics and generally deplorable deportment. 'What did he mean about his wife? I didn't know he had one.'

'Oh, yes, he has one. She just doesn't live with him any more.'

Suspicion made Holly narrow her eyes and then lower her gaze to the deep jade of the oriental carpet. 'I see. And what does that have to do with you?'

'Nothing. Or nothing I could do anything about. Gloria's a silly woman and she drinks too much. She made a pass at me at a party once. Domingo overheard, and assumed I was attempting to seduce her.'

'And weren't you?'

His eyelids drooped, but not before she'd seen a bright flicker of contempt. 'No, my dear, I was not. Strangely enough, other people's wives aren't my forte. Unfortunately, though, the resultant brouhaha didn't do a lot for their marriage.'

'Oh.' Holly thought of apologising, and then remembered she was under no obligation to apologise to a man who had kidnapped her and very probably lost her her job.

'The point,' Ethan continued after a pause, 'is that your friend has been anxious to pay me back ever since. So he made sure your progress through London's more ostentatious establishments was well-reported, and programmed his staff to reveal your whereabouts in case I should happen to enquire. I imagine the idea was to make me believe he'd seduced you. It seems he had some insane idea that I —'

'That you cared?' suggested Holly, with a high, unnaturally brittle laugh. 'How absurd.' When Ethan only regarded her through enigmatic, half-closed eyes, and failed to respond, she added brightly, 'And how do you know he *hasn't* seduced me?'

'If he has, he did a very poor job of it. You don't look to me like a woman who's been awakened to the delights of the bedroom.'

Holly had always regarded violence as an immature way of handling anger, but from the moment she'd met Ethan he'd had the effects of overturning all her most ingrained beliefs. Now she locked her fingers firmly behind her back before she could do anything unwise, and leaned into the softness of the cushions. 'That's none of your business, is it?' she replied coolly.

'Not the least,' he agreed with an amiable smile. 'The business I have in mind is of a practical, though, I must say, much less stimulating nature.'

Holly willed herself not to react. Ethan would explain himself when, and if, it suited him. In the meantime she saw no sense in playing his game.

He watched her for a few seconds with an expectant little gleam in his eye, but when she didn't respond he remarked casually, 'I've just given Willoughby the sack.'

'Have you?' She flicked a loose thread off her skirt.

'Mmm. I want you back, Holly.' He leaned his head against the bookcase, drawing her gaze to the taut, muscular column of his throat.

'To work for you?' she asked cautiously. There was no point allowing herself to hope.

'Yes, of course.'

'But we've already been over all that,' she said, as a great weariness made her shoulders sag.

'I know. And I should never have let you go in the first place.'

'How do you think you could have kept me?' She eased her hands out from behind her. 'Is there a secret torture chamber attached to your office or something, where you persuade reluctant secretaries to do your bidding?'

Ethan's mouth tipped up wryly. 'Thanks for the suggestion,' he drawled. 'It may come in handy some time. For instance if I can't get you to — er — do my bidding . . . did you say? . . . by more conventional methods.'

'Such as?' asked Holly, not quite as weary any more.

Abruptly Ethan moved across the room and lowered himself on to the seat beside her. When his knee brushed against her thigh she edged as far away from him as she could get.

'Such as giving you more money, telling you I need you, promising not to lay a finger on your charming person . . . '

Oh, if only he'd lay a whole lot more than a finger on her, thought Holly despairingly. He was so achingly, fatally desirable . . .

'You already did all that,' she said, her voice strained.

'So I did. All right. Any other ideas, short of thumbscrews or boxing your ears?'

'Those wouldn't work either,' said

Holly. 'They're also illegal.'

He grinned, and Holly wished he wouldn't, because his grin made her go warm all over.

'It wouldn't be the first time I've broken the law.'

'Maybe not. But it still wouldn't work.'

Ethan sighed. 'I was afraid it wouldn't. That leaves me with only one alternative.'

'What's that?' asked Holly warily, not trusting the determined glitter in his eye.

'Oh, persuasion of the usual kind.' He loosened his tie, stretched out his legs, and gave her a calculated and very sexy grin.

'What?' She pulled at her belt and shifted uncomfortably on the cushions. 'Oh. I see.'

'Do you?'

'Yes. You think you've got me where you want me, don't you?'

'And where do you imagine I want you?' His voice was low and unbearably seductive.

'Well, I . . . ' Holly bit her lip and tried to convince herself that she hadn't meant what she knew he thought she'd meant.

'I wasn't talking about bed,' he said, trailing his finger absently down her cheek. 'Although I admit that idea does have its charms.' When she looked up with an anxious start he added softly, 'Nor was I planning to strip you down and starve you into submission. As a matter of fact, I was hoping good old-fashioned flattery would do the trick.'

When she didn't answer, his heavy eyebrows rose in sardonic amusement. 'But I suppose I could do a nice Bluebeard if I'm pushed. Is that what you think of me, Holly Adams?'

At this moment Holly didn't know what she thought. She was only aware of his long arm stretched along the back of the love-seat, and of his firm fingers just inches from her neck. She lowered her eyes.

'No,' she said doubtfully. 'I suppose not.'

'Then come back to work for me. It's not like you to be so contrary, and playing hard to get doesn't seem your style.'

He spoke so impassively that Holly felt a painful tightening in her chest. Ethan didn't know what her style was, because he'd never taken the trouble to find out. And she had a feeling that she might not be at all hard to get if he moved much closer . . .

But of course he wasn't talking about the heat pulsing low in her stomach. His concern was the inconvenience of being without a competent assistant.

'I'm not being contrary,' she replied, in a voice that, to her horror, started out brisk and breezy and ended up choking on a sob. 'I'm being . . . ' She stopped, unable to finish.

'Difficult,' finished Ethan, with sudden harshness. 'There's no need to cry. I do want you back, of course, but not at gunpoint.'

'I'm not crying,' said Holly, wiping the back of her hand across her eyes.

'You could have fooled me. Here.'

He held out a clean handkerchief, but, when Holly didn't take it, and before she could stop him, he had pulled her hand away and was busy mopping her cheeks. She swallowed as his fingers curved firmly round the nape of her neck.

'That's better,' he said when he'd finished. 'Now what was that all about?'

His knees were just touching hers, his body was bent towards her, and there was something in his eyes that commanded honesty. 'I'm not ... I wouldn't be ... hard to get,' she murmured, so softly that Ethan could barely hear her.

His eyes narrowed, and suddenly the room seemed alive with a dangerous kind of static. 'Ah. I see. Well, well.' He drew back to get a clearer view of her face, and the hand that still circled her neck sent a series of tingling shivers down her spine.

He studied her for several seconds with a hard, inquisitorial gaze that made her feel as if he suspected her of extortion. But when his scrutiny was completed he slid his thumb across her back and said crisply, 'All right. Let's get back to the business in hand.'

'What business?' Holly glared at him, confused and unnerved by his odd behaviour. 'And would you mind unhanding my neck?'

'Not at all.' He dropped his arm at once, and lounged back against the arm of the love-seat. 'Obviously I was referring to the matter of your employment.'

'I'm staying with Hall and Goodman,' Holly said quickly.

'I suppose that may be an option. I'd prefer you to come back to me.'

'Why? So you can treat me like a doormat again, and forget that I exist except to shout at?'

'My dear Holly, the fact that I could forget your existence, yet know that my affairs were running smoothly, was precisely why I found you so invaluable.' The corner of his lip turned down. 'And I only shouted at you when you pushed me sorely.'

'David never shouted at me,' said Holly.

'Very forbearing of him.' Ethan spoke coldly. 'In case you haven't noticed, I'm not David.'

Oh, she'd noticed all right. For one thing, she'd never felt the smallest desire to hit David — or to wrap her arms around him and fall with him on to the big, soft cushions . . .

'Exactly,' she said hastily. 'That's precisely why I find you so impossible.'

He laughed, but there was no light of laughter in his eyes. '*Touché*. What else did David do to earn your undying devotion?'

'He behaved like a gentleman,' snapped Holly, resenting the mocking lift to his voice.

'Oh, yes? As opposed to what?'

'As opposed to a Neanderthal,' she retorted.

'Ah. So that's it. You never did explain why you left me. I knew I shouldn't have roused my Sleeping Beauty from her virginal slumber.'

'That had nothing to do with it,' lied Holly, not sure if she was more hurt by his gibe at her virginity, or delighted that he had called her a beauty.

'Didn't it? In that case, I fail to see the problem.'

She shrugged. 'There's no problem. *I'm* going back to work for David, and you — '

'And I am going to see to it that you don't.' His brow smoothed out and he began to strum his fingers on his thigh.

Holly moistened her lips, her gaze on the tight pull of cloth as he stretched his legs. 'How do you propose to do that?' she asked finally. 'By sheer bullying?'

'If all else fails.' He tipped his head to one side and grinned suddenly. 'Stop being so damned obstructive, Adams, and do as you're told.'

'Nice try,' said Holly. 'It won't work.'

'OK. How about we go back to plan one? You told me you wouldn't be hard to get — and I can only assume that means you wouldn't object to working for me again. So state your terms.' He spoke briskly, as if the subject was beginning to lose interest for him.

'Ethan . . . ' Holly searched for the right words and didn't find them. 'Ethan, I don't want to work for you again. Ever. It's over.'

Ethan crossed his legs and went on strumming. 'Is it? But if you're not hard to get . . . '

'When I said that, I wasn't talking about coming back as your assistant.'

'Ah.' He glanced at her sharply. 'I see. I did wonder . . . As what, then?'

'As . . . I don't know, I suppose — I've never slept with a man, Ethan . . . ' She stopped, horrified. Gazing into the hard brightness of his eyes, she couldn't imagine what had made her tell him that. She lowered her head and began to fumble with the corner of a cushion.

'I see,' said Ethan again. 'So that's it. And of course you're not suggesting I should take immediate steps to remedy that unfortunate oversight?'

'Oh!' Holly jumped to her feet, stung by the coldness of his voice and the disdainful implication that any such suggestion was ridiculous. 'Do you really think . . . ?' She took a deep breath and started again. *'Please.* I wouldn't dream of demanding such a sacrifice.'

He ignored her outburst and nodded calmly. 'So that *is* it. I might have guessed.'

'Guessed? Guessed what?'

'That little Miss Adams knows what she wants and goes after it. Something to do with a wedding-ring, I imagine.'

His voice had turned so cold and taunting that when Holly's gaze fell on the dull gilt frame of one of his priceless pictures she longed to tear it from the wall and break it over his supercilious head. Instead she clasped her hands in front of her until her knuckles turned white, and said icily, 'I hope you don't imagine I want *your* wedding-ring, Ethan. And I certainly have no desire to join you in your bed. Or in your office, for that matter.'

'Oh, I think you could be persuaded into accepting at least one of those options, if I decided to — er — make the sacrifice.' He linked his fingers loosely behind his head. 'But on the whole I don't think I will. You see, I've travelled this route once before, and I never make the same mistake twice.'

Holly put a hand over her eyes. 'I *don't* see,' she said. 'And, what's more to the point, I don't care. I'd like you to take me home now, please, Ethan.'

He laughed without mirth. 'You mean I went to all this trouble for nothing?'

She didn't answer, and his hard gaze travelled slowly from her face, which she knew had gone deathly pale, to the fingers she gripped so tightly at her waist. Then it moved back up again. When their eyes met for the second time, Holly thought she saw a shade of doubt fracture the cold arrogance of his appraisal. But it was gone almost instantly, and she decided she must have been mistaken.

'Very well,' he said, rising so swiftly that she took a hasty step backwards. 'I get the picture, as they say. Where's your coat?'

'I wasn't wearing a coat when you . . . when you kidnapped me.'

'Your bag, then,' he said, ignoring the angry blaze of her eyes.

Holly picked up the bag, which had fallen off the arm of the love-seat, and Ethan followed her over to the lift.

It wasn't until they were seated in his car that he spoke again, and then it was only to remark lightly, 'So much for my efforts to replace Willoughby. It's just as well I'm not in Personnel.'

Holly could only agree dully that his hiring practices did indeed leave a lot to be desired.

He stopped outside her gate, but, when she reached for the door-handle, all at once she felt his hands on her arms. Then he was pulling her around, and she was gazing up into his heavy-lidded eyes. Bedroom eyes, she thought, hypnotised by the hungry frustration that electrified the confined space of the Maserati. It was a frustration Ethan was no longer troubling to conceal from her. Or from himself, she supposed.

'Ethan . . . ' she murmured, her own body recognising his need.

Ethan said, 'Hell,' moved his arms to her waist, and dragged her into his arms.

Instantly all the sensations she had experienced before came rushing back, and, even as she fought to resist, she surrendered to the contagion of his touch. His kiss was searing, brutal, and his hard hands played up and down her spine, over her hips, causing her to strain towards him as she succumbed to the rapture of a need stronger than any she had ever known or dreamed of. It was as if his tongue, probing her willingly parted lips, her knowledge of his arousal, and the intoxicating feel of his tough body pressed against her own, were her only reason for being.

But when she gave a soft, delirious moan, suddenly Ethan held her away and, breathing heavily, said, 'There. That ties things up nicely, then, doesn't it? You have now become far too distracting to keep around the office, and I have become too much of a jerk to work for.' He turned away from her and laid both arms on the wheel. 'Goodbye, Holly.'

Holly stared at the ungiving hardness of his profile, at the pulse beating strongly in his neck, and, to her disbelieving confusion, she was suddenly overcome with a profound tenderness for this difficult, hard-bitten man who had kissed her with so much passion before pushing her harshly out of his life.

She touched a tentative hand to his cheek. But he flinched away and glared straight ahead at the street. A small boy riding past on his bicycle caught a glimpse of his rock-hard face and almost toppled on to the asphalt.

Slowly Holly dropped her hand, whispered, 'Goodbye, Ethan,' and stumbled out on to the pavement. She walked up the path like a robot, and when she reached the door she looked back.

Ethan was sitting with his head bowed over the steering-wheel. He stayed like that for a few moments, then she saw him start the car with swift, angry motions, and roar down the street and out of sight.

The next day she reported to Hall and Goodman as usual, and David, looking smug, said that of course he had paid no attention to Ethan's high-handed resignation of her job.

She went back to work feeling as if she had survived a hurricane only to land up in a black hole. It was as if all the feeling had been sucked out of her on that sunny afternoon in Ethan's flat. She didn't know what had happened, why he had suddenly decided it was a wedding-ring she wanted more than him. And sometimes she thought that had nothing to do with the way he'd behaved. It was almost as if all at once any excuse would have done as long as it got her out of his orbit.

She found herself walking through each day like an automaton, smiling when she was expected to smile, nodding sympathetically or sagely when the need arose, and assuring everyone that yes, she was entirely satisfied with her job, thank you, and life couldn't possibly be better. And it was true. You couldn't be sad if you weren't able to feel.

Then one Saturday near the end of June the feeling came back.

She had just removed Chris from the kitchen sink, where he was mixing up a concoction of milk powder, orange pop and junket, and was about to remove the cats from the sitting room, where they were contemplating fresh fillet of goldfish, when she glanced up to see the front gate swinging open.

It was Ellen, looking about fifteen in a shocking pink sundress that totally eclipsed her pale, ethereal features.

Holly closed her eyes as the memories she had locked away came flooding back.

Heronwater. Colby Yorke's cold blue eyes, and Ethan's warm brown ones smiling at her over the rim of his glass. Ethan assuring her that he happened to like mushrooms. Ellen telling her that her brother was interfering and bossy and that they would do a lot better without him . . .

But she wasn't better without him. As she watched Ellen trip jauntily up the path, it came to her in a devastating revelation, almost like a blaze of light from on high, that the knowledge she had shied away from for months could not for a moment longer be denied.

She loved Ethan. He was a handsome man, just like all the other handsome men she had known and successfully avoided. Yet somehow he had managed to melt the protective shell she had grown to shield her heart. He was no different from the rest, though, as she had instinctively known all along. Oh, he had been kind to her in an offhand way, when it suited his needs, dismissive and overbearing when she failed to march to his tune, but . . .

No. He wasn't like the others.

Ethan had kissed her not because it was expected of him, but because he wanted to, and even though he had promptly denied its importance his kiss had brought her to life. And somewhere in between that first kiss and the moment she saw Ellen running up the path she had discovered there was more to love than kisses. She loved Ethan for the kindness he didn't often show, for his decisiveness and for his laughter — and even, God help her, for his arrogance.

For the first time Holly realised that, in spite of her loving family and friends, she was desperately lonely and alone.

Ellen's knock reverberated through the house, and she ran to answer it with feet that seemed to fly across the floor.

'Ellen! Come in. What a surprise. I . . . ' She stopped, overcome with a sudden puzzling shyness.

But Ellen didn't notice. She laughed, and swept into the house as if she owned it. Then her eye lit on Chris, who was gazing up at her with his thumb in the corner of his mouth. 'Hello, who are you?' she asked, beaming at the wary little boy. 'Do you live here too?'

Chris nodded. 'With my mummy and daddy and Annie Holly,' he volunteered.

'I'm babysitting,' explained Holly. 'Barbara and Noel have gone shopping. Would you like some tea?'

'Love some.'

Holly went to put the kettle on, but it wasn't until Chris had been put to bed for his afternoon nap that she was able to concentrate on Ellen, who was standing over the goldfish, watching it swim.

'You can't figure out why I'm here, can you?' She smiled and sat down in the nearest jumble-sale armchair. Her smile reminded Holly poignantly of Ethan.

'No, I can't. But I'm glad to see you.'

'Are you? I thought you mightn't be.'

'Why ever should you think that?'

'Well . . . ' Ellen lowered her long, pale lashes. 'The thing is, Ethan's always been one to button up his feelings. But he's been about as much fun as frost at a picnic lately, and when I happened to mention your name the other day he told me he didn't want to talk about you.' She fixed Holly with a bright, perceptive eye. 'So I thought maybe *you* were the reason he's suddenly become so impossible — '

'He was always impossible,' muttered Holly, forgetting for a moment that she was talking to Ethan's sister.

Ellen laughed. 'I know. But he's worse. He and Dad have never been all that close, and now they can't seem to agree about anything. Dad's even threatening to go back to work, and the doctor says he mustn't.' She frowned. 'I don't know quite why, but somehow I have this idea you can help.'

'Me?' Holly's mouth fell open. 'But

you said Ethan won't even talk about me.'

'He won't, and he's got this gorgon doing your job now who won't let me speak to him on the phone.'

'Does she make his coffee?' asked Holly, surprised to hear her words come out in a croak.

'Oh, yes. Ethan calls her Private Jenkins. Says she's very good at taking orders. I suppose he's the sergeant.'

'Field Marshal,' murmured Holly.

Ellen chuckled. 'Yes, you're right. Holly, will you come to dinner tomorrow? At Heronwater.'

'To dinner? But why? I mean . . . ' She reddened slightly and started again. 'I'm sorry, you must think me terribly rude, but I don't understand. Surely if . . . I mean, surely I'll only make things worse.'

Ellen shook her head. 'No, you won't. You couldn't. The thing is, Dad expects me to be there most Sundays, and it's been absolute murder lately. Boyd won't come with me any more.'

She took in Holly's puzzled frown, and added ruefully, 'I suppose that's not much of an invitation, is it? Can I start again?'

'Yes, of course, but I don't see . . . ' Holly sneezed and gave up. She had a feeling that, when it came to getting what she wanted, his sister was every bit as much of a tyrant as Ethan.

Ellen crossed her elegant ankles. 'You see, Ethan's always been a bit of a loner. He's maddeningly independent, you know, and totally determined to do things his way. When he wants something, he just reaches out and takes it. He was close to our mother, I think — but she died. When we were children he used to say she'd deserted him, and the truth is, Dad's always lavished most of his attention on me — which Ethan says hasn't done me a bit of good.' She grinned. 'He's probably right. Anyway, he was usually left with no one to rely on but himself, so he's never really let anyone get close to him. Except maybe once.' She paused, and wrinkled her forehead. 'The thing is, his kind of tough self-sufficiency may have worked fine in Canada, and again when he took over in London. But if you ask me, he's finally reached for something he can't have. I'm not sure he even knows he wants it, but, all the same, it's driving him crazy.' She sighed. 'Not to mention the rest of us.'

'I know the feeling,' said Holly. She got up and walked over to the window. 'But Ellen — I don't see what you think I can do.'

'Mmm.' Ellen eyed her pensively over the rim of her teacup. 'Maybe you can't do anything. It's just an idea of mine. Will you give it a try?'

Holly stared at the unkempt lawn with its cheerful profusion of butter-cups and daisies, and she wondered irrelevantly if Noel had got the mower fixed yet. What was Ellen asking her to do? Was she suggesting that she, Holly, was the 'something' Ethan wanted but couldn't have? No, that couldn't be. If Ethan had put his mind to it, he could have got her to do anything he asked. He knew it too, and yet he'd given up his attempt to get her back into his office as if she'd suddenly turned into one of the leggy sirens he so abhorred. And now he had Private Jenkins, so all his problems were solved.

But hers weren't. She wanted Ethan, and Ellen was offering her an opportunity to see him. She had nothing to lose by accepting. Except her heart, she thought dismally. And that was already lost.

'All right.' She turned away from the window. 'Thank you. I'd like to come to dinner tomorrow. But don't expect miracles, Ellen. I'm not much good at taming dragons.'

'Oh, Ethan's no dragon. Or if he is, he's breathing ice instead of fire.' She stood up. 'Anyway, that's settled. I'll be here to pick you up about twelve. Is that all right for you?'

Holly nodded and sneezed again. She had a feeling Ellen would arrive at twelve whether it was all right for her or not. The Yorke siblings had more than they realised in common.

The next day she was ready by eleven, wearing a cotton dress with a pattern of orange daisies, and a white sunhat with a wide orange band. She didn't much care if she got freckles, but she had an idea that the hat might provide useful protection from hazards more dangerous than the sun.

Ellen was late, which didn't surprise Holly, but the speed with which they reached Heronwater did. All the same, it wasn't speed that made her heart beat faster when they pulled up in the front courtyard with a screech of brakes just as Colby Yorke appeared in the doorway. It was the thought of seeing Ethan again.

'Hello, Daddy, I've brought Holly.' Ellen jumped out of the car and ran to embrace her father.

Holly, stifling a sneeze, followed her and extended a tentative hand. Colby took it with more warmth than she expected, and she was about to tell him how pleased she was to see him again when a movement at the top of the steps caught her attention.

Ethan, dressed in navy trousers and a cream-coloured shirt, was staring down at her as if he didn't believe what he was seeing. And just for a moment she thought she saw his eyes light up as if the sun had come out from behind a cloud.

Then his eyelids dropped down like shutters and his face went blank, and Holly knew the cloud would bring a storm.

8

'Hello, Ethan,' said Holly, going up to him. 'Didn't Ellen tell you I was coming?'

He shook his head, and she knew that only an iron control was enabling him to maintain his impassive façade. His coldness tore at her heart. It was nearly a month since she had seen him last, and she sensed a hardness in him that hadn't been there before. He had always been strong and self-contained, but this was different. It was as if he had consciously erected a wall of steel between himself and the rest of the world.

'No,' he said, taking her arm. 'She didn't. If she had, I wouldn't have been here.'

Holly felt the tight band of restraint inside her snap. Once his rejection would only have hurt her. Now resentment overrode the pain.

'How gallant of you,' she said, as he led her through a labyrinth of passageways to a paved terrace at the back of the house. 'Tell me, Ethan, do your charming manners come naturally, or did you take lessons in how to make guests welcome?'

He laughed without warmth. 'You aren't welcome. Why did you come?'

'Because Ellen invited me.'

'You could have refused.'

'Why should I refuse? She particularly wanted me to come.'

'I wonder why,' he mused softly. 'Ah. Here she is now. Have a seat, Holly.' He pulled out a wooden *chaise-longue* and helped her on to it. Ellen sat down opposite on a deck-chair.

'See what I mean?' she muttered, when Ethan went away to fetch drinks. 'He's horrible, isn't he?'

Holly saw what Ellen meant all right, but she didn't think Ethan was horrible. She thought he was the most spectacular and desirable man she had ever

252

known. And she had missed him desperately. It was no consolation at all that for the past month he had apparently been getting up on the wrong side of his bed. She was about to impart an expurgated version of this opinion to Ellen, when he returned carrying a tray of drinks.

Colby soon joined them, and, after making a few politely social remarks to Holly, he turned to his daughter and began to question her minutely about her doings since he had seen her last week.

Holly watched Ethan stretch his long legs and settle himself in a deck-chair. She hadn't often seen him like that, so casual and sinuous and sexy. Her gaze moved to the wide leather band of the wristwatch circling his muscular forearm, and she shifted restlessly. When she became conscious that she, the watcher, was being watched, she looked up and saw that, although he appeared to be looking at her, she couldn't really tell, because his eyes were hidden behind dark glasses.

Feeling ill at ease and miserable, and wishing she hadn't come, Holly lay back, tipped her hat over her eyes, and allowed the sun to soak into her skin. Next to an unrestricted view of Ethan's seductively sprawled body, she would have preferred to enjoy the peaceful vista of smooth lawns sloping down to the willows beside the river, and to watch the light flickering brilliantly through the leaves. But Ethan's unreadable gaze was too disturbing. She knew he was annoyed with her for coming, but she didn't really understand why, and she wasn't about to give him the satisfaction of observing how much his coldness had hurt her.

In spite of her deep unhappiness, or maybe because she needed to escape, Holly had almost drifted off to sleep when his voice pulled her up sharply. 'Holly? Dinner won't be for another twenty minutes. Come for a walk.'

Holly sat up with a jerk and glanced quickly over at Ellen and her father.

'They're absorbed in their weekly news exchange,' he explained. 'Come on.' He held out his hand. Instinctively she took it, and felt her fingers spark at his touch.

A few minutes later they were strolling along a narrow path beside the river.

Just like a couple of summer lovers, thought Holly bitterly, although there was nothing lover-like in the strong grip of Ethan's hand.

'All right,' he said. 'Now tell me what this is all about.'

She stopped, and looked up at the set planes of his face. 'It's not about anything,' she said evenly. 'If you must know, Ellen thought my presence might improve the atmosphere at your dinner-table.'

'Ellen's head was always on back to front.'

'Thank you,' said Holly. 'I'm glad to see your disposition hasn't changed.'

'Holly . . . ' He took her arm and pulled her round to face him, and she saw that his eyes, minus the glasses now, were alight with an emotion that was part anger and part dangerously controlled frustration. 'Holly, it's not going to work.'

'What isn't?' She frowned, genuinely puzzled.

'I'm not letting you set me up for a fall.'

'Look,' said Holly, pulling her arm away, 'I've no idea what you're talking about, and I don't like riddles. How in the world could I set you up for a fall?'

'It's been done,' he said cryptically. When she continued to stare at him as if she doubted his sanity he growled, 'I told you before. I never make the same mistake twice. So stop wasting your time.'

'What mistake?' asked Holly. 'And if you don't give me a straight answer, Ethan Yorke, I'll — '

'What will you do? Throw yourself into the river? Try it, and I may let you drown.'

'I'm sure you would,' she said coldly,

as something frozen and hard settled painfully over her heart. There was no point in continuing this conversation. Ethan was convinced she had some devious plot up her sleeve. What it was, she had no idea, since she'd let him know, convincingly if not quite truthfully, that he had nothing to give her that she wanted. But it was obvious he didn't trust her, and without trust there couldn't possibly be love. She had come to Heronwater today because she wanted to see him again, to find out if there was reason to hope — as Ellen had seemed to think there might be. But Ethan was probably right: Ellen did have her head on backwards.

She turned away and began to walk back to the house.

'Where do you think you're going?' he rasped, closing a hard hand over her shoulder.

'Away from you.' She kept on walking.

'Given up, have you? Wise girl.'

'I've given up on you, if that's what you mean.'

'What else should I mean? You offered yourself to me, didn't you? Presumably in the expectation of future benefits. Unfortunately for you, that game has already been played.'

Holly stopped dead. She still wasn't sure what he was talking about, but she was sure she'd just been insulted. Heaven knew, she'd had enough practice in shrugging off unintentional insults. This one was intentional, and she wasn't going to shrug it off. This time she was going to strike back.

Taking a deep breath, she swung round, raised her arm, and aimed a well-placed blow at his face.

Ethan caught her wrist long before she found her mark, and jerked her forward until her forehead was almost touching his chin. 'Nice try,' he said softly. 'You missed.'

'Oh!' Furiously Holly tried to twist herself out of his grasp, but he was smiling now, that cool, implacable smile she knew so well. And he wouldn't release her.

She struggled some more, but she might as well have been struggling with a rock for all the good it did. Finally she gave up and stood still, her chest heaving.

Immediately Ethan let her go, and she staggered back and wrapped her arm round the trunk of a willow tree. Staring down into the weeds, she felt unexpectedly giddy. But the bark was rough, and it chafed her bare arm, so with a soft exclamation she loosed her hold.

Water lapped gently at the bright green banks of the river, and Holly gazed down at it, mesmerised. She leaned forward, thinking she saw a flash of silver in the blue-green depths, and as she bent over her foot caught in the willow root.

The next thing she knew, silver had flaked into a million broken facets of light, and cold blue-green was rushing over her head.

'You didn't have to take me so damn literally.'

Holly opened her eyes. She seemed to be lying on the riverbank. She was cold and wet in spite of the hot sun burning overhead, and Ethan was kneeling over her. His face was very close, and he didn't look hard and contemptuous any more; he looked . . . distraught. But the moment he saw her glaring at him, distraction changed to relief and . . . was that *amusement* she saw in his eyes?

Amusement! How dared he be amused when she had almost drowned?

'I didn't take you literally,' she snapped. 'I slipped. Surely you didn't think I'd try to drown myself over you?'

He shook his head. 'No. Frankly I didn't. Do you know you look remarkably like a waterlogged duck?'

'I doubt if ducks get waterlogged,' said Holly, sidetracked, as he had meant her to be. Then she added caustically, 'I thought you said you'd let me.'

'Let you what?'

'Drown.'

'Ah. But that was before I saw you take a nosedive into your sunhat and come up looking like a mermaid. Here are your glasses, by the way.' He took them out of his pocket and slipped them over her nose.

'Nobody's ever called me a mermaid before,' said Holly, even more side-tracked, and focusing on the delicious outline of his lips.

'Haven't they?' Ethan touched her cheek, and for a moment he didn't seem amused, or impatient or angry, or any of the emotions she had come to expect. If she hadn't known better, Holly would have sworn he was as confused and hopeless as she was. Without thinking, she reacted to the hunger in his eyes and looped her arms round his neck.

At once he froze. She felt his muscles go rigid, and knew she had done the wrong thing. 'I'm sorry. It's cold,' she said, quickly releasing him. 'Would you help me up?'

'Of course. I wasn't planning to let you dry out in the sun.' He stood up in one smooth movement and scooped her into his arms. 'Put your hands back where they were,' he ordered. 'Those wet clothes make you about as easy to hang on to as a porpoise.'

The moment of vulnerability was over. 'Thanks,' said Holly, swallowing. 'I liked being a mermaid better.'

'Mmm. I liked you better as a mermaid myself.'

He started to stride towards the house, and Holly, knowing that this would be the only time he would hold her like this, surrendered to the bliss of resting her head on his shoulder and lying close to the heart of the man she loved. She could feel it beating hard through his shirt.

'Did you rescue me?' she murmured. 'Everything was so confused. One minute I was looking at the water, the next my hat fell off, and after that I don't exactly remember.'

'After that you surfaced like a bedraggled mermaid, and I pulled you out. I suppose you might say I rescued you.'

'Oh,' said Holly. 'But you're not even wet.'

He stopped in his tracks. 'No. Disappointed? If you like, I'll throw you back in and we can start again.'

He's losing patience, thought Holly. And if he wasn't wet before, he soon will be. She could see that the dampness from her dress was beginning to soak through his shirt.

Suddenly she sneezed, and Ethan quickened his pace.

'You're not catching a chill, I hope,' he said, as if it were an accusation.

'You don't hope it nearly as much as I do,' replied Holly. Then she added grudgingly, 'But I suppose I could be. I've been sneezing a lot.'

She didn't hear his reply, which was just as well.

A minute or two later the coolness of the house closed around her, and she saw that Ethan was carrying her up a narrow, curving staircase she hadn't noticed before. Somewhere in the background she heard Ellen's laughter ring out. It was followed by the sound of applause.

Ethan swore and said, 'Damn Ellen.'

Holly was inclined to agree. She didn't want him reminded, by his sister or anyone else, that carrying her masterfully up the stairs as he was doing might present a hopelessly misleading picture to the world.

A few seconds later he shouldered open a heavy oak door and tipped her upright.

'Right,' he said. 'Off with that dress.' He strode across to a monstrous dark-panelled wardrobe and began to rummage through a selection of clothes. When he turned around, holding a garment made of soft white towelling, and saw that she was standing exactly where he had put her, he repeated gruffly, 'I said off with it. You're shivering. Do you really want to catch your death?'

'No.' Holly's teeth began to chatter. 'But I can't — I'm not undressing in front of you.'

'Such maidenly modesty. Do you imagine I've never seen a woman take her clothes off?'

'No — and I expect you did the taking off.' She shivered again as a wave of nausea swept over her. That dunking in the river must have done more damage than she'd thought.

It wasn't until she felt Ethan's hands on her shoulders, firmly pushing down the straps of her dress, that she realised exactly what she'd said.

'Don't,' she cried, trying to push him away. 'I didn't mean — '

'I don't suppose you did, but you're right. I've done my share of undressing, and I've no intention of letting you stand here and pass out at my feet.' He pushed the dress down over her hips until it fell in a heap on the dusty pink carpet. Then, without so much as

265

batting an eyelid, he reached round to unhook her strapless bra and allowed it to follow the dress.

'Now put this on,' he commanded, draping the white towelling garment around her shoulders. 'And get that slip off at once.'

Holly slipped her arms into the robe and fastened the belt with fingers that weren't at all steady. After that she did as he said, and turned her back on him before tugging down her clinging wet slip.

'Panties,' snapped Ethan.

Holly gulped and pulled those off too.

'OK,' he said. 'Now you'd better have a bath to thaw out. I'll fetch Ellen.'

'No,' said Holly quickly. 'There's no need to trouble Ellen. Just show me the bathroom.' She turned to the door, stumbled, and almost fell.

'Don't be ridiculous.' He put an arm around her. 'There seems to be more wrong with you than there should be after nothing more than a tumble into the river on a sunny day. I'm not leaving you alone in the bath.'

Holly smiled wanly, and, because he was right, and she wasn't feeling herself, she giggled and replied, 'Aren't you? Is that a threat or a promise?'

'Take it any way you like.' He turned her around, led her past a huge four-poster bed with a cream quilted cover, and lifted her up a step into a bathroom containing the biggest shell-pink bath-tub she had ever seen. She looked again. It was solid marble.

'Now,' said Ethan, 'do I fetch Ellen, or do you want me to stand guard at the door?'

'But it must be your dinnertime,' she hedged.

'Dinner will wait. Well? Which is it to be?'

'Ellen,' said Holly in a small voice. She wasn't up to arguing with Ethan. Not when she felt weak all over and as if her head were about to split in two.

'Fine. Sit down.' He waved at a wooden bathroom chair, and Holly sank into it thankfully.

In a moment she heard voices at the door, and Ethan telling someone to fetch Miss Yorke. Then he was back in the bathroom, glaring down at her, with both hands grasping the door-jamb above his head.

Holly said nothing — it seemed safest — and a couple of minutes later Ellen appeared.

After that she didn't remember much beyond warm water swirling round her in the bath, subtly scented soap, and Ellen fussing over her in what she had once heard Ethan call her 'mother-duck' voice.

When she woke up, she was lying on her back in the four-poster. The curtains were drawn — rich cream velvet, she noticed — and Ethan was standing beside the bed, scowling down at her as if she were Goldilocks and he an irate Father Bear.

'What time is it?' she asked, sneezing. 'I'd better be going . . . '

'It's six o'clock and you're in no

condition to go anywhere.'

'It's only a cold,' said Holly, sneezing again. 'Along with a bit of a headache — and a funny feeling in my stomach.'

'Flu,' said Ethan. 'I had it myself. You'll be all right in a couple of days. Meanwhile you're staying in bed. I'll send for some supper.'

'Oh, I couldn't eat anything. Where's Ellen?'

'Gone back to London. She's done her damage for the day. And Dad's just left for Scotland. There are one or two golf courses up there.'

'You don't say.' She stared at a pattern of leaves carved into the centre of the ceiling. 'When are you leaving?'

'I'm not,' he said grimly. 'I'm the designated nursemaid.'

'Oh, but I'm all right. You don't have to — '

'I know I don't have to. I choose to. My fool sister, who was responsible for bringing you here, says she has an urgent appointment in town. With Boyd and a bed, I imagine. That leaves me to uphold the family tradition of hospitality. We'll start with supper.'

'But — '

'No buts, Holly,' he said wearily. 'Just do as you're told, and I'll restore you to your brother's tender care the first moment I can.'

He sounded so worn-out, and so disgusted with the burden thrust upon him, that if Holly had felt better she would have leaped out of bed and left Heronwater in her nightgown rather than do as she was told. Unfortunately she didn't think she could walk.

She spent the next two days in the four-poster, being waited on by an attentive staff. It was a new experience for her. As a child she had almost never been ill, and on the odd occasion when she'd had a cold, Noel had invariably had one too, so she had had to share her mother's gentle fussing with her twin. At Heronwater there was no sharing.

Ethan saw to it that she had the best of everything, including a TV set and anything she wanted to read, but his own visits to her room were brief, and usually merely to assure himself that she was eating whatever bland invalids' food he had decreed should be her dish of the day. But he flatly refused to return to his office, saying he didn't like unfinished business and would see this task through to the bitter end.

When Holly told him she didn't like being referred to as a bitter end, he only laughed — which was an improvement on the grim expression he usually wore.

On the Tuesday, she made up her mind to tell him she was going home. There was no point in prolonging the agony. And it *was* agony, lying in bed waiting to hear his step in the corridor, hoping he might look at her with tenderness, but seeing only cold impatience on his face. He didn't love her. He never would, and she had been a susceptible innocent even to think for a moment that his kisses had been more than a careless impulse brought on by a couple of drinks and a party in one case, and sheer bad temper in the other.

But at least in those days he had liked her most of the time. She didn't think he did any more. That afternoon at his flat had changed everything. Now he treated her as if . . . as if he almost despised her.

Holly frowned and sat up straight in the bed. Damn it, she hadn't done anything to deserve his contempt, and before she left he owed her an explanation. Oh, he had made sure she was looked after when she was ill, had even seemed to care for her a little. But he had no right to treat her with less respect than she'd seen him bestow on Barbara's cats.

That evening when Ethan came into the bedroom he found Holly sitting in a pretty chintz armchair wearing her neatly washed and pressed sundress. Her hands were folded tightly in her lap.

'I'm going home tomorrow,' she told him, her gaze fixed on his feet. 'But before I do, I want to know what I've done.'

'Done?' His deep baritone stirred her senses unbearably. 'Nothing fatal. You've inconvenienced me a bit, but I can hardly hold that against you.'

'That's not what I mean.' Holly took a deep breath and made herself look him in the eye. 'What . . . what did *you* mean that day in your flat when you implied I wanted a wedding-ring? Which I don't. And the other day, when you said you wouldn't let me set you up for a fall. Ethan, why have you been treating me like a . . . ?' She hesitated.

'Gold-digger on the make?' he suggested, bending over her and gripping the arms of her chair. 'You mean you object to that classification? If the shoe fits, wear it, my dear.'

9

Holly gasped, and let out a little cry of shock. His face, cold and pitiless, was only a few inches from her own. She tried to draw away, but her head hit the back of the chair.

'How dare you?' she said, her voice a furious whisper on the air. 'I don't want your gold, Ethan. Did you really imagine I was offering you the use of my body in exchange for money and security? You know what that would make me, don't you?' When he didn't answer, but continued to stare at her with eyes that were hard and enigmatic as brown glass, she bowed her head and finished dully, 'I suppose that answers my question. Will you move, please? I'd like to get up.'

She felt rather than saw him move away, and, without looking at him, she stood and walked over to the window.

Between the leaded panes she watched the sun cast long shadows across the lawn. There were heavy purple clouds on the horizon, and as she gazed frozenly up at the sky she recognised that soon they would bring rain.

She didn't care. Ethan had given her the answer she'd demanded of him, and that answer had wounded her as no physical blow could. It was as if he had taken her heart into his hands and crushed it until there was nothing left for him to hurt — or for her to feel.

'Holly?' His voice, too close to her ear, sounded loud in the high-ceilinged room. 'Holly, I didn't imagine for a moment that you'd settle for a temporary affair. So you can stop acting as if I'm a fate worse than death. Obviously it had to be marriage.'

Holly felt his breath warming her cheek, and she swung around to escape him. But his body was blocking her way, his strong hands on the window frame behind her.

'Please let me pass,' she said frigidly,

her gaze on the open neck of his shirt. 'I have to find my bag. I think I'd better leave right away.'

She waited for him to move, but when he didn't she was forced to raise her head.

He was looking at her with eyes so bleak and empty that they frightened her. 'You're not leaving,' he told her, as though there was nothing more to be said. 'I'll return you to your brother tomorrow — with your virtue intact.'

Suddenly she was no longer frightened, and the anger and the pain she had been bottling up, because she was afraid she would explode if she gave them rein, refused to be contained a moment longer.

'You will not return me to Noel,' she said furiously. 'You will not do another damn thing for me, Ethan Yorke. And you can't keep me here against my will, because if you do I'll start screaming. However devoted your servants may be, I doubt they'd ignore a woman screaming rape. As for my virtue, you're quite right that at the back of my foolish little mind I hoped for marriage. But if you'd asked, I'd have given myself to you without question — *and* without any strings. What's more — '

She didn't get any further, because Ethan placed a hand across her mouth. 'I get the idea,' he said. 'May I ask you *why* you would have made such a sacrifice? Some kind of penance, perhaps?'

Holly stared at the grim line of his mouth, at the anger in his eyes which rivalled hers . . . and the need to hurt him as he was hurting her became overpowering.

She parted her lips and bit hard into the tough palm across her mouth.

Ethan swore, and put his injured hand on the small of her back to jerk her up against him. 'You really are anxious to do penance, aren't you?' he said softly. 'I'll be glad to oblige. But first of all I want to know why. Why me, Holly? Why no strings?'

She felt his firm hand slip down

below her waist, curving over her bottom, and she was unable to stifle a gasp as the old hunger overcame even this terrible pain and indignation. She knew then that although she would never see Ethan again after today she would always long for him. And pride didn't matter now. She would tell him what was in her heart, and, even though he wouldn't believe her, or care if he did, she would know that she had told him the truth. There would be no lies or misconceptions between them, and she would be able to leave this house in some kind of peace.

'Because I love you,' she said.

She felt him stiffen, and then he held her away, gripping her by the elbows as his narrowed eyes searched her face for confirmation that she meant it.

He studied her for a long time, until at last, with a strangled groan, he let her go.

'Dear God,' he murmured. 'You're telling the truth, aren't you? Or you think you are. What in the hell have I done?'

There was blood on his palm, and a small spot stained the collar of his shirt.

'I hurt you,' said Holly, instinctively reaching out to touch him.

He flinched, and put a hand over his eyes so that she couldn't tell what was going on in his head. Not that I ever knew, she thought drearily, as she walked across to the bed and sat down.

'Not as much as I hurt you.' His voice, low and rasping, made her look up quickly. He was staring straight ahead, not seeing her, or the room, or the deepening shadows on the lawn. 'I'm sorry, Holly. I didn't know.'

'It doesn't matter,' she said. 'Hadn't you better do something with that hand?'

He glanced down, seemed surprised to see the blood, then shrugged and went into the bathroom. She heard water running, and in a little while he was back. His hair was wet and she supposed he must have run it under the tap.

He stopped just outside the door and propped himself up against the wall.

'We have to talk,' he said.

'Yes? Do we?' Her fingers plucked at the cream-coloured quilt.

Ethan rammed his hands into his pockets. 'Yes. I'm afraid so.'

'What's to talk about? I said I love you; you said you're sorry. What else is there to say?'

'You have the right to know why I jumped to the wrong conclusion. I have an obligation to explain.'

'I told you it doesn't matter,' said Holly tiredly.

'I think it does.'

She heard the note of finality, knew that even if she leaped to her feet and made a run for it Ethan wouldn't let her go until he'd done what he felt had to be done. And she was too tired, her heart was too heavy, even to make the effort to run.

'All right,' she said. 'Explain.'

280

Ethan closed his eyes. When he spoke it was all on one level, as if he knew that if he broke off or paused for emphasis he wouldn't be able to go on.

'You remember Alice Adonidas?' he said, not waiting for her to answer. 'Ten years ago she worked for Smart and Yorke. I was just down from Cambridge, beginning to learn the business, and Alice was assigned as my secretary. She was a clever girl, good at her job — and very lovely . . . '

'Distracting,' murmured Holly.

His mouth turned down. 'Very. I fell in love with her, and she fell in love with me. Or so I thought. She was the first woman I'd ever seriously cared for. Oh, I'd known a few girls at Cambridge — and before that — but I'd never fallen for anyone the way I fell for Alice. She made me feel as though I was the most important person in her life. That was a new and heady pleasure for me. To the rest of the world I was Colby Yorke's son. To my father I was Ellen's brother. To Alice I was Ethan.'

He didn't sound quite so controlled now, and Holly stopped plucking the quilt to glance at his face. She remembered what Ellen had said about his second-place childhood. His eyes were bleak, looking back to a time when he'd been young and vulnerable — when the mother he loved had died, and the father he had never been close to sent him away without giving him time to adjust.

'I wanted Alice desperately,' Ethan went on. 'But she always held me off, said she was saving herself for the man she married. I knew my father would be furious if he knew about us. He wanted me to concentrate all my energies on learning the business before I even thought about settling down. And for once I agreed with him. But although Alice said she understood, all she would allow me were a few chaste kisses — until the day my youthful hormones got the better of me, and I proposed. After that we were officially engaged.'

'And your father was furious?' asked Holly. She felt profoundly sorry for the lonely young man who had been Ethan, but she still didn't see what he was leading up to, or what difference this tale of youthful passion could make to her.

'Oh, yes. But there wasn't much he could do.'

No, there wouldn't have been. Even at the tender age of twenty-two, Ethan with his mind made up must have been a force to contend with.

'In the end, though,' he said grimly, 'he didn't have to do anything. Alice was suitably compliant in bed, and I was too besotted to acknowledge even to myself that something was missing. But one day I came back unexpectedly from a meeting, and discovered my intended and Ron Rakow, our advertising manager, having a passionate coffee-break on my desk. They didn't know I was there, and I heard her tell him I was a stuffy, work-obsessed bore, but that she was going to have to marry me because she'd been poor all her life, and she didn't mean to be poor any more.' His mouth curled in an ugly grimace. 'As you'll have noticed, she isn't. Adonidas soon stepped in to take my place. Rakow was merely a diversion.'

'Poor Ethan,' said Holly, pulling off her glasses. She was beginning to see now where this was leading, although she didn't see what it could change.

Ethan's harsh laugh scraped at her overwrought nerves. 'Don't waste your sympathies on me, Holly. Ron ended up in the hospital for a week. He eventually withdrew an entirely justifiable assault charge in exchange for a very large settlement. Alice was the one I should have assaulted — and no doubt would have if Ron hadn't got in the way. I'm not proud of that episode.'

Holly saw his fists bunch at the constraint of his pockets. 'You've no reason to be,' she said, replacing her glasses. She still felt as if there were an iron band wrapped around her chest, and Ethan's past transgressions weren't her problem.

'I agree.' He wiped a damp hand across his face. 'In any case, my father decided I'd better do my apprenticeship in Canada, well away from the inevitable gossip. I didn't argue. Why should I? It was a sensible decision. He was always sensible.'

'As you are now. Usually. Ethan, I'm sorry your first love turned sour on you, but . . . ' Her voice cracked suddenly. 'But what does it have to do with me? Why are you telling me about it?'

He closed his eyes for a moment, and Holly saw deep, bruising shadows underneath them. 'I'm trying to explain,' he said wearily. 'It wasn't just my first love that turned sour. I suppose you could say I turned sour on love itself. I no longer allowed myself to indulge in that passionate obsession. And I shan't marry. As I've no particular desire to hurt anyone, I try to date women whose emotions aren't likely to become involved. It's proved a satisfactory arrangement up to now — until somehow you slipped between the cracks.'

'I'm sorry,' said Holly. She wasn't, and she hoped her sarcasm was obvious.

'So am I. When I hired you, I saw you as the ideal assistant: efficient, relatively obliging once I had you licked into shape — ' his guard dropped for a moment and he seemed to smile ' — and above all, undistracting.'

'In other words, dull and uninteresting,' said Holly, trying to sound as if she didn't care.

Ethan sighed. 'Not at all. I've told you before that habit you have of belittling yourself will one day cause some employer with a short fuse to wring your delectable neck. I've frequently been tempted myself. You're not dull, Holly, you're smart and capable. And you have a most delightful smile. I wouldn't have kissed you if I hadn't found you attractive.' He put his fingertips up to massage his forehead.

'But that's where our troubles began, isn't it?'

'I suppose so,' said Holly. She hadn't thought of the kiss as trouble at the time.

'So you see,' he said, raising his head, 'when you made that crack about not being hard to get, I thought I'd found myself another Alice-on-the-make. It was a natural enough assumption in the circumstances. You'd already refused to come back to work for me, and any fool could see you weren't the type to go in for transitory affairs. I'm not a fool, Holly. So for a man who knows love is a myth, what else was left?' His mouth twisted. 'I was as angry with myself as with you, though, because I've always been so damn careful to avoid that particular situation.' He crossed the room, sat down beside her on the bed, and took her hand. 'Hell. I didn't mean to hurt you . . . You know that.'

Holly looked up at him through her green glasses, and her eyes were swimming with tears. She choked them back. He might not have meant to hurt her, but he had. And it was all very well for him to unburden himself and assume that an apology made everything all right. But it didn't. She felt numb now, but soon the numbness would wear off. Then the pain would begin again in earnest. Hopelessly, she wondered if it would ever go away. Snatching her hand from Ethan's, she stood up.

He thought she was just some foolish little woman who had fallen in love with the boss. An inconvenience who could be shrugged off with explanations, and dismissed with a sigh of relief.

But as Holly stared down at the dusty pink carpet, it came to her that she couldn't really blame him. He had no special reason to feel responsible. He hadn't asked her to fall in love, hadn't for a moment been aware that she had. And how should he be? She'd refused to acknowledge it to herself. For some reason, that only made it worse.

'I forgive you,' she snapped over her

shoulder. 'And don't flatter yourself. I may just manage to pull through.'

'I've no doubt you will,' he said quietly. 'You're strong, Holly. And I'm a very curable affliction.'

'Yes. But that doesn't mean I can stay here another night. I have to go home, Ethan.'

He came up behind her and, taking her by the shoulders, turned her firmly around. 'Don't be an idiot. If you're feeling better you can have supper with me, then I'll drive you home in the morning. Surely you can bear with me for one more day?'

One more day. And after that there wouldn't be any more days. Holly wasn't sure if she *could* bear it. But when he put it to her in that bracing, confident tone, as though he couldn't believe she had so little courage, it was a challenge she had to accept.

'All right,' she said, plastering a bright smile on to her face. 'I suppose I can put up with you if I must.'

'For a woman who professes to be in

love, you're remarkably hard on a man's ego,' he observed.

He spoke as though it didn't matter, but there was a look in his eye that . . . No. She mustn't think along those lines. He was teasing her. But it was a cruel teasing, and if he stayed in this room one moment longer she'd start to scream.

'Go away,' she said. 'I'll join you for supper, but right now I'd like to be alone.'

He raised his eyebrows, ran his knuckles over her chin, and said, 'Of course. I'll see you at seven.'

As Holly watched him walk across the room and out of the door, she wondered if it was true that hearts could break.

When she turned to look out of the window, it was raining.

Supper, to her surprise, wasn't as unbearable as she'd feared. Ethan, when he chose to make the effort, could be charming, and he entertained her with amusing anecdotes about Smart and Yorke and about his life in Canada, and made no reference to their earlier conversation.

Holly, also making an effort, managed to smile and nod and force all thoughts of the morrow from her mind. The meal, light and delicately flavoured, was served with quiet discretion by the young woman who had brought her meals while she lay in bed. When the coffee came, Ethan suggested they should retire to the sitting room where they had sat that first time she'd come to Heronwater.

They talked desultorily, then, when they ran out of conversation, Ethan said, 'I'll have breakfast sent up to your room at seven, if that suits you.'

She nodded. So they weren't to have breakfast together. It was just as well.

Silence fell between them, and Holly was just about to say that she thought she'd better get an early night when the phone rang.

Ethan rose lazily and loped across the room to pick it up from its perch on a small mahogany table beside the window.

She sat watching him through her lashes, and in a moment she saw a slow smile spread across his face. 'Jeanie!' he said. 'How nice to hear from you.' There was a pause, and then he murmured, 'I've missed you too.'

Holly felt a sudden burning behind her eyes, and she stood up quickly and hurried out of the room. Obviously Ethan was talking to one of his 'women whose emotions aren't likely to become involved'. It sounded as though this emotionless liaison was going fine.

She wiped a hand over her eyes and decided that, after all, she couldn't take another night in this house. It would be hell to lie awake for hours, knowing that in the morning Ethan would drive her into town and out of his life. Better to leave now, while he was on the phone, and she still had the strength of mind to follow her instincts. Because she knew that if she waited to say goodbye he would only insist that she stay. And when Ethan insisted on something, it happened.

She ran upstairs, grabbed her bag and the cardigan she had brought to put over her sundress, and, without anyone seeing her, managed to slip out of the front door.

The driveway stretched ahead of her, and it was raining. She knew she shouldn't get wet so soon after having the flu, but it was a warm night in spite of the rain, and she had seen a bus-stop half a mile down the road. She had no idea how often the buses ran, but there was bound to be at least one more tonight — and the stop was under cover.

Buttoning her cardigan up to the neck, and wishing her sunhat hadn't floated down the river, she took a long breath and started to run down the driveway as if Ethan and the entire Heronwater staff were in pursuit.

But no one pursued her — no one even saw her — and she reached the stop out of breath, very wet, and alone.

To her enormous relief, the bus came only ten minutes later.

At about the same time as Holly reached the bus-stop, Ethan put down the phone and went to find her. When she wasn't in her room, he searched the rest of the house and then the garden. After that he returned to her bedroom and noticed that her bag and every other trace of her had gone.

Feeling as if something had cracked him hard in the chest, he ran downstairs and out into the rain. He reached the bus-stop just in time to see the bus pulling away. When the spray from its back wheels soaked his trousers, he slumped against a tree and put an unsteady hand up to still the angry pounding in his head.

He hadn't felt like this, he realised with frustrated fury, since the day he had walked in on Alice and Ron.

'Holly,' he grated under his breath, 'if you've been fool enough to go home in this weather with nothing on but a sundress and a sweater, so help me, you deserve to get pneumonia. And if I could get my hands on you at this moment, believe me, you'd get a hell of a lot more than that.'

10

It was after eleven by the time Holly arrived back in Chiswick. Barbara, who was already dressed for bed, took a look at her sister-in-law's face and said, 'My God, what did the man do to you? Apart from trying to drown you, that is.'

Holly smile wanly. 'He didn't try to drown me. Actually he sort of rescued me from the dangerous waters of the Thames.'

'Well, he should have sort of seen to it that you stayed rescued. You look like a refugee from my mother's fruit and broccoli punch. And I know the feeling. Noel, get Holly a brandy.'

'There isn't any.' Noel's head emerged from the kitchen. When he took in Holly's white face and dilapidated condition, he groaned. 'Dear lord. I hope I'm not supposed to challenge that fellow to a duel.'

'Don't worry,' said Holly. 'I wasn't compromised.'

She sounded so woebegone that Barbara looked at her sharply and muttered, 'Which was obviously no cause for celebration.'

Holly sneezed, and Barbara and Noel exchanged glances as they moved with one accord to take her arms.

'Bed,' said Noel, as the two of them led her up the stairs. 'Hot-water bottle, hot chocolate and lots of sleep.'

Holly nodded, too tired to argue, although she was certain that in spite of her exhaustion she wouldn't sleep. The memory of Ethan's rigid face as he'd told her that he didn't indulge in love — which he'd referred to with scorn as a 'passionate obsession' — was bound to keep her awake. And she knew that in her mind she would go over again and again her last glimpse of him: smiling as he told a woman called Jeanie he had missed her.

Twenty minutes later, as Holly lay in

her single bed, staring into the darkness, the telephone rang. She blinked. Who on earth could be calling at this hour? Should she answer it? No, Barbara already had it. Her soft voice was a faint murmur in the night.

She turned on her side. Her skin felt very warm now, but inside her everything was cold. Perhaps it always would be. Maybe she would always feel hollow, as if the very core of her being had been siphoned out . . .

'Unless you can die when the dream is past . . . ' The words of Elizabeth Barrett Browning's beautiful love-poem drifted into the emptiness of her mind.

No! She sat up suddenly and glared at the pale path of a moonbeam. No. She was not going to die. The dream was past, and now it was time to dream a different dream. A survivor's dream. In the morning she would get up, go to work, smile, and pretend that everything was fine. And some day, years down the road perhaps, everything *would* be fine. She would forget Ethan, and learn to be happy in her cottage with her cats.

Cats? Instead of Ethan? If she hadn't felt so much like crying, Holly might have laughed. Instead she buried her face in the pillow and squeezed her eyes shut. However hard it might be, she was *not* going to allow herself to be kept awake by the memory of a man and a kiss. Even though that man was Ethan . . .

In the end it wasn't memories that kept her awake.

It was a raging fever.

When morning came, Barbara took one look at the unnatural brightness in Holly's gold-flecked eyes and ran to the phone to call a doctor.

* * *

Holly sat in solitary state in the sitting room, watching the goldfish go round and round in its tank. It was the first time she'd been downstairs in almost a week, and Barbara had taken Chris to visit friends so that his annie Holly could have some much needed peace.

Chris didn't understand about convalescence. He was quite sure that if Holly was resting quietly in a chair she must be anxious to be sat on, climbed over or coaxed into energetic games of hide-and-seek.

Barbara had tried to explain that people who had just recovered from pneumonia needed quiet, but quiet wasn't a word in Chris's vocabulary.

'It's all right,' Holly had remonstrated weakly. 'I don't mind.'

'No, but I do.' Barbara's reply had brooked no argument, and the moment the clock on the mantel struck two she had whisked Chris out of the house as if she thought another moment in the little boy's company would send her sister-in-law into a decline.

Whatever a decline is, Holly thought wearily. If it's anything like this horrible, dreary nothingness that makes me feel like a very ancient turtle, I think I'm already in one.

She didn't remember much of her illness. Fluids and a lot of fussing were the two things that stuck in her mind. Then this morning the doctor had said she was much better and there was no reason why she shouldn't get up. So she had put on her faded green cotton robe and settled herself in front of the goldfish tank with a book that she had no desire to read. The trials and tribulations of fictional lovers couldn't seem to hold her attention. Besides, for them there would be a happy ending, and she didn't believe in happy endings any more.

For her there hadn't even been a happy beginning, she thought sadly. Her love had begun and ended with Ethan's kiss.

A shadow fell across the window, but when she looked up there was no one there. She opened her book without interest, and immediately a heavy fist started hammering on the door.

Holly sighed. Did the postman *have* to make so much noise? She got up and walked slowly into the hall, relieved to find her legs felt much stronger.

The hammering started again, and she winced. By the time she had the door open, she was beginning to fantasise about how satisfactory it would be to scalp a certain employee of the Royal Mail.

Only it wasn't an impatient postman who stood on the step looking like the big bad wolf attempting to blow down the house.

As she would never in a million years have guessed, it was Ethan.

Holly stared blankly at the formidable, dark-suited figure with his hand poised to demand instant admittance. Then, as sensation returned to her limbs, she moved to shut the door in his face.

Ethan promptly inserted his foot so she couldn't close it.

'Oh, no, you don't,' he said. 'I've had about all I'm going to take from you, Holly Adams.'

'You don't have to take anything

from me,' said Holly, who was beginning to think she must be dreaming. 'In fact I'd prefer that you didn't. So if you'd kindly remove your shoe — '

'I have no intention of removing my shoe. And I'm not about to let you slam the door on me.' He rested his shoulder against the wooden frame, crossed his arms, and appeared quite prepared to remain there till hell froze over — or till Holly opened the door. Whichever came first, she supposed.

That was when she knew he was no dream. Every nerve in her body had begun to sing, because she realised she would have to let him in. Then the singing ceased as she took in the look in his eyes, and saw that her troubles were not over. There was danger as well as excitement in that look. His features were stern, and his gaze flicked so disparagingly over her worn green robe that for a moment she wanted to turn tail and run. Except that she couldn't run yet, and in any case Ethan would follow her. There was determination as well as a kind of controlled forbearance about the tough body waiting calmly for her to move.

Holly gave up and stood back. At once he stepped across the threshold and kicked the door shut behind him. After that he put his hand on her shoulder and marched her ahead of him to the sitting room.

Holly turned round and eyed him warily. Her heart was thundering in her ears, and she wanted desperately to throw her arms around him. At the same time, she wanted to wipe that look of icy restraint off his face.

'Why have you come?' she asked. 'It's obvious you're not pleased to see me.'

'Is it? The feeling seems to be mutual.'

'No.' Holly shook her head. 'I would be pleased to see you if I didn't get the idea you'd like to . . . ' She hesitated, searching for words.

'Punish you?' he suggested. 'For running out into the rain and driving me half crazy with worry? Nothing would give me greater pleasure. Unfortunately you're not up to it yet. And in any case, I don't have the right.'

'I'm glad you realise that,' said Holly. 'So why *did* you come?'

Ethan's eyes shifted to the goldfish. 'To reassure myself, I suppose.'

'About what?'

'About you, you ridiculous woman.' He took her by the arms and glared down into her face. 'What the hell did you mean by running out on me?'

'I didn't run out on you,' said Holly in a frozen voice. 'You didn't want me, remember.'

He groaned, and twisted a hand through her hair. 'Oh, I wanted you all right. I didn't want a *wife*, but that doesn't mean I had any wish to be responsible for your death.'

So that was what this was all about. Ethan didn't want her on his conscience.

'As you can see, I'm not dead,' she said stiffly. 'You could have found that out over the phone. In any case, now that you've managed to soothe your guilt pangs there's no need for you to waste any more time. Is there? I'll see you out.'

'Oh, no, you won't.' His grip on her arms tightened. 'That's not all I came for, my dear. Although I freely admit it was part of it.' He took a deep breath. 'Why did you do it, Holly?'

'Why did I do what?'

'Lord give me strength,' he muttered. 'Why did you run away?'

Holly's moistened her lips. Her legs felt mushy again, and all of a sudden she couldn't meet his eyes. 'I need to sit down,' she told him.

'Of course.' She was surprised to hear the quick compassion in his voice as he helped her on to the serviceable brown sofa and began to arrange cushions behind her back. But as soon as he had finished he sank down uninvited beside her and demanded as if there had been no interruption, 'Well?'

There was no point in pretending she

306

didn't understand him. 'I ran away because I heard you talking to someone called Jeanie, and I just couldn't bear it any more. If I'd told you I was leaving, you'd have tried to stop me.'

His smile was cool. 'No, I would not have tried to stop you. I'd merely have done it.'

'That's what I mean.'

Ethan pushed a hand through the burnished brown hair she was desperately longing to touch, then asked grimly, 'Do you mean to tell me you actually preferred death to one more night in my house? Jeanie, by the way, is an engaging but eccentric old lady who lives in the flat below me in London. I sometimes pick up cat food or cigarettes for her. She phoned to tell me she was back from a visit to her daughters and wanted me to bring her a tin of something repulsive called 'Puddy Pie'.'

'Oh,' said Holly, tugging at the belt of her robe and trying not to smile at the expression of revulsion on Ethan's face. 'I didn't mean — '

'Yes, you did. But it doesn't matter. Go on.'

Holly stared at the deep blue pattern of his tie. 'I don't think I was thinking in terms of death,' she admitted finally. 'I just had to get away from you.'

'Charming.' He touched the back of his hand to her cheek. 'I suppose it didn't occur to you that I might just wonder where you were?'

'Well, yes, it did. Later. But I didn't think you'd care.'

'You didn't think I'd care that a guest in my house, who was still recovering from the flu, chose to take her chances with pneumonia rather than endure my company for one more night? Holly, if that's the kind of man you believe I am, what on earth made you decide to fall in love with me? Or am I right in thinking that your flight from Heron-water signalled the end of a temporary and very curable passion?'

Holly heard the hard note of strain in his voice, saw something snap in his eyes that she didn't think she'd seen there before — and for one wild, ecstatic moment she believed he wanted her to tell him that it hadn't ended, that her passion was alive and well and living in this room. Then common sense reasserted itself, and she managed to say with just the right touch of lightness, 'Passionate obsessions are very boring, aren't they? Of course I'm cured.'

To her astonishment, instead of heaving a sigh of relief, Ethan frowned and said coldly, 'I congratulate you.'

'Ethan . . . ' Holly hesitated. He was acting so strangely this afternoon, almost as if he didn't want her to be cured, as if he wanted her to go on loving him — to go on hurting. She pushed herself up on the cushions as pain and resentment added strength to her voice. 'Ethan, I don't need your congratulations. I don't need your company. As to what made me fall in love with you — I've no idea. It happened when I wasn't looking. But I'm looking now, and I don't care at all for what I see. So will you please leave? Now. And next time you have a twinge of conscience, send a donation to charity.'

She started to get up, but Ethan caught her wrist and pulled her back down beside him.

'I'm not leaving,' he said.

Holly felt a current shimmer up her arm and settle in the pit of her stomach. 'Please,' she whispered, her gaze on the bunched knuckles of his fist. 'Please, Ethan. There's really no more to be said. If my running off like that worried you, I'm sorry. But it's not likely to happen again.'

'No.' He fixed her with a commanding brown eye. 'You're damn right it's not. Holly . . . ' He paused and when he spoke again his voice had changed. It sounded raw, as if he found it hard to get the words past his throat. 'Holly, did you mean it when you said you had — shall we say — *recovered* from the misfortune of loving me?'

'Oh, for the love of . . . ' Holly

couldn't go on. For the love of Ethan, *of course* she hadn't recovered. Did he really think her emotions were so shallow? And why was he tormenting her like this?

'Holly?' he persisted. 'I want an answer.'

Oh, he wanted an answer, did he? And what Ethan Yorke wanted, he got. Even if it wrenched at her heart, and left her exposed and bleeding to the eyes of the uncaring man who had brought her to this miserable pass.

All right, if he wanted an answer, she would give him one. Right between the eyes.

'Yes,' she bit out through her teeth. 'Yes, I meant it when I said I'd recovered. I meant it to save my pride. I wanted to be able to look at myself in the mirror and know that I hadn't really fallen for a man so cold and self-centred that there was no room in his heart for anything but his own needs and wishes — and certainly no room for love. That would mean reaching out to someone else, wouldn't it? Having to think of someone besides yourself. Naturally I wanted to recover from such a futile, unintelligent attachment.' She lowered her head, suddenly defeated by the mysterious blaze of light in his eyes. 'I meant it,' she went on in a different, quieter voice, 'but of course I lied.'

'What are you saying?' All at once Ethan's hands were on her elbows, holding her so she couldn't pull away. 'Tell me the truth, Holly. I need to know.'

The fight went out of her then. She raised her eyes to his face and said dully, 'The truth, of course, is that I haven't stopped loving you. I don't suppose I ever will.'

Ethan let out his breath on a long sigh. She hadn't even realised he was holding it.

A rueful, indescribably sensual smile brushed across his lips, and before she knew what he was about he had taken off her glasses and was pressing her back against the arm of the sofa. Then he was kissing her as if he never meant to stop.

For just an instant, Holly resisted. Then the feel of his body on her own, of his hands in her hair, his mouth on her mouth, moving, tasting, all combined to make her forget that she had vowed to forget this man — to make a life for herself in which he could never have a part.

With a soft cry she put her arms around him and surrendered to the ecstasy of his kiss. She felt his firm thigh ease between her legs, and she gave a gasp of delight as ripples of pleasure shot through her body. But when she moved her hands to his chest and started to unbutton his shirt he groaned softly, pushed her arms to her side, and sat up.

Holly lay still and stared up at him with the wide, vulnerable eyes of poor sight. Without her glasses she didn't know if he was angry, indifferent or elated.

'Ethan . . . ?' she murmured.

He lifted her fingers to his lips. 'Holly,'

he said gruffly, 'my sweet, guileless, wonderfully honest Ms Adams, do you think you could possibly revive a futile, unintelligent attachment and give a cold and self-centred man another chance?'

Holly struggled up on the cushions, reached for the glasses Ethan had put on the coffee-table, and peered doubtfully into his face. There was no anger there, no indifference or elation, only a deep sincerity and need. And . . . could that be apprehension she read in the fierce brightness of his eyes?

Did he really fear her rejection? She was almost afraid to find out.

'Another chance to what?' she asked warily.

Ethan put his head in his hands and groaned. 'No commitment without detailed facts and figures, is that it? All right, then, I want another chance — no thousands of other chances — to kiss you, to make love to you, to make up for all the hurt I know I've caused. To put it concisely, Ms Adams, I want to marry you.'

Holly swallowed, gazing in amazement at the warm glow of tenderness in his eyes. But she saw that the muscles in his jaw were drawn tight, and there was a thin film of sweat across his brow. Why, he really means it, she thought, in a bemused haze of wonder and disbelief. He really wants me to say yes.

She opened her mouth, meaning to say it, but instead of speaking the words she knew he was waiting to hear, a sudden quirk of mischief made her pause, 'And do you always get what you want, Mr Yorke?' she asked him primly.

Ethan frowned, doubt and uncertainty giving a hard edge to his features. Then, to her consternation, he stood up, nodding as if she'd confirmed his worst expectations. When he began to make for the hallway, Holly cried out, 'Wait! Ethan wait. Please don't go.'

He swung round, took a long look at her face, and then said slowly, and with dawning understanding, 'No, I don't always get what I want. But I'm going to get it this time. Aren't I, Ms Adams?

And if you dare say no, I'll — '

'What will you do?' asked Holly, holding out her arms.

'I'll kiss you and put you to bed.' Ethan crossed the room in two strides and put the first part of his threat into action.

'I think,' said Holly after a while, 'that in that case I may as well say no. The alternative might not be as nice.' She wrinkled her nose. 'What is the alternative?'

'More of the same and forever.' He pulled her on to his knees and pushed back the front of her robe.

'Oh. That's even better.' Holly busied herself with the buttons of his shirt, then laid her head on his bare chest and said with quiet certainty, 'Yes.'

Ethan gave a triumphant laugh and tipped her back on to the cushions. After that he allowed his lips to begin a slow and purposeful exploration of her neck, her breasts, the silky smoothness of her stomach and, again, the welcoming sweetness of her lips.

It proved to be remarkably distracting.

'Why are you stopping?' asked Holly some time later, when quite suddenly he sat up, put her glasses back on her nose, and began to pull her robe around her shoulders. 'I don't want you to stop.'

'I know. Neither do I. None the less, we will wait. Until our wedding night. Which will be memorable.' He threw her a tip-tilted grin and started to do up his shirt.

Holly frowned as all her old insecurities came flooding back. Didn't Ethan want to make love to her? Was he marrying her out of some misguided sense of knight-errantry?

'You didn't wait until your wedding night for Alice,' she pointed out. 'Ethan, you don't *have* to marry me, you know.'

Ethan stopped fastening his shirt and turned to face her. 'Do you think I would if I didn't want to?' He smiled at her with a grave tenderness that was unusual for him. 'Holly, I love you. It's *because* you're not Alice that I won't take you right here and now in your brother's house.'

Reluctantly Holly sat up. Ethan loved her. The words exploded in her head. At last the man who had sneered at love as being nothing but a 'passionate obsession' had fallen victim to that obsession himself. When he had asked her to marry him, she had known instinctively that his feelings ran deep, even though he hadn't openly said so. But what did he mean about Alice? What had Alice to do with this hot July afternoon when she longed so desperately to take Ethan into her arms and make him hers?

'I don't understand,' she said finally.

'I know. How could you?' He scooped her up and settled her back on his knee. 'Considering that a week ago I told you I no longer believed in love and would never marry, I'm amazed, and eternally grateful, that you didn't react to my proposal by turning me out of the house.'

318

Holly smiled. 'You wouldn't have gone,' she said simply.

'True.' He grinned. 'But you had every reason to try. Holly, darling, if I've made you unhappy these past months, it may be some consolation to you to know that I've been through hell and back this last week. When you disappeared into the rain like that, I honestly thought I'd go out of my mind. At first I was just worried, then, after I phoned your sister-in-law and knew you were safely home, I got angry. Later they told me you had a severe case of pneumonia. That's when I really went off my head.'

'You didn't look worried when you turned up at the door this afternoon,' remarked Holly, smoothing a finger over the creases in his forehead. 'You looked murderous.'

'I was. Your family said I shouldn't try to see you before you'd recovered, in case I caused a relapse.' He cocked an eyebrow at her. 'Not very complimentary, that. And it left me with a whole week to come to the conclusion that I'd been a total fool. I think I knew all along that you were no gold-digger, but I didn't want to admit it even to myself. I'd been burned once before, you see, and after that it seemed much safer to look on all women as a potential threat to my mental health. In other words, I was so blinded by my memories of Alice that I almost allowed the world's most desirable mushroom to get away from me.'

'That's not very complimentary either,' said Holly, pursing her lips.

'Yes, it is,' he replied, kissing them. 'I told you I'm devoted to mushrooms. The point is, it wasn't until I realised there was a chance I might actually lose you that I finally understood what I should have known all along: that I loved you. I don't think I was looking either. But you see . . . ' He closed his eyes, and as Holly gazed at him lovingly she saw a deep weariness, and lines of care that hadn't been there before.

She knew then that Ethan had

suffered as much as she had.

'I suppose,' he went on after a long pause during which she could have sworn she heard the beating of their hearts, 'that I've been fighting that love, and you, from the moment we met. That's why, when I finally got around to kissing you — '

'You behaved like a bad-tempered bear.'

'Did I? Yes, I suppose I did. I hadn't learned to trust again, you see.' He smiled, and, picking up her hand, blew gently into her palm. 'Life was much simpler before I met you, Ms Adams. Simpler — and infinitely emptier. Then, when it was almost too late, it dawned on me just what it was I was throwing away — '

'So you decided it was all my fault,' said Holly drily.

'Don't be cheeky.' He ran his hand down her spine until it came to rest deliciously on her rear. 'It was certainly your fault you caught pneumonia. And I *was* ready to murder you for that. But

I suppose I'll have to wait till you've recovered.' He grinned, and tugged gently at a lock of her fine hair. 'Holly, I've spent a great many years convinced that all attractive women under sixty, with the exception of my scatter-brained sister, were grasping little sirens like Alice. Can you understand that because you're *not* Alice — ?'

'Yes,' said Holly, smiling into his eyes. 'I understand perfectly that, because I'm not Alice, the next few months are likely to drive me crazy.'

'Weeks,' said Ethan, smoothing his hands slowly over her hips and making her gasp. 'We'll be married as soon as we decide on a date and place. And if it makes you feel any better, those weeks will drive me crazy too. So let's begin working on it now.' He rolled her off his knee, stretched her out on the sofa, and began very systematically to do just that.

When Barbara and Chris arrived home half an hour later, Barbara took in the dishevelled couple hastily rearranging their clothes on her sofa, and smiled smugly. 'I'm not sure that's *quite* what the doctor had in mind when he recommended a quiet convalescence,' she remarked with her nose in the air.

Chris, never one to mince words, wanted to know if Mr Yolk had a red mouth because he'd been trying to eat his annie Holly.

It took them another half-hour, and several lollipops miraculously produced from Ethan's pockets, to extricate themselves from that one.

★　★　★

Ethan stalked into his office and stopped dead.

At six o'clock on Christmas Eve he had expected to find the building deserted. He had only dropped in to pick up the gift he'd been hiding from Holly — a topaz necklace that matched the gold of her eyes — and at this moment he wasn't exactly bursting with festive feelings. After a frustrating hour stuck in traffic, all he really wanted to do was get home, collect his wife, and head straight for Heronwater. This year he was looking forward to the family Christmas in spite of Ellen's lame ducks and lame-brained boyfriend, because Holly would be with him to share the burden — and the joy and laughter.

But at three o'clock an unexpected problem had come up at one of the suburban shops, and that, followed by a traffic jam, and now an unexpected intruder in his private office, was not calculated to enhance his seasonal spirit.

'What the devil do you think you're doing?' he demanded of the figure bent over in his chair.

A head slowly emerged from beneath the desk. 'Good evening, Jacob Marley,' said Holly, sitting up straight. 'Are we caught in a time warp, or does Christmas Eve always have this disarming effect on your temper?'

Ethan felt himself begin to relax. Holly always made him feel human again when he was ready to start cracking heads or terrorising staff. How had he ever managed without her?

Grinning, he ran a hand through his hair and replied, 'No. I think *you* have the disarming effect, my darling. Is it too much to ask what you're doing under my desk?'

'Looking for the mistletoe,' she explained, with an innocent smile that made him want to shake her.

'I don't hang mistletoe on the floor.'

'Well, no, but I lifted some from Payroll and I dropped it.'

'I see. Were you planning for me to kiss Private Jenkins? I'd much rather not.'

Holly giggled and held the errant mistletoe over her head. 'No, I was planning for you to kiss me. I knew I'd find you here. Last year you made me enter data on Christmas Eve, but I wouldn't want it to become a habit.'

Ethan put his briefcase on the floor, swung round the desk, and removed the mistletoe from her fingers. 'I don't need any dried-up plant life to make me kiss you,' he said firmly, taking her hands and pulling her on to her feet. 'Happy anniversary of our meeting, Mrs Yorke.' He extended his arms and attempted to pull her up against his chest.

But almost at once he gave up, and cast a dubious look at her waistline. 'There aren't any triplets in your family, are there?' he asked with an exaggerated shudder.

'No,' said Holly. 'But there will be after April. That's what I came to tell you. I've just been to the doctor, and she says — '

'What?' Ethan swung away from her and strode across to the window. 'Did you say . . . ?' He put his hands behind him and leaned on the sill for support.

Holly was nodding at him, her golden eyes round with anxiety. 'Is it . . . ? Don't you want . . . ? I mean, aren't you pleased?'

'Pleased?' He wiped a hand round the back of his neck and discovered it was damp. 'Pleased? Holly, darling, I am astounded, dumbfounded, confounded and overwhelmed. Yes, you might say I'm pleased.' He held out his arms.

'I'm glad,' said Holly, going into them. 'I was afraid you might think three was too many.'

'Oh,' said Ethan. 'You mean I have a choice? In that case I'll have two boys and a kitten.'

'No, you won't,' replied Holly. 'You'll have three girls — called April, May and June.'

He shook his head. 'At that I do draw the line.'

'All right, how about Rose, Iris and Primrose? Or Ruby, Opal and Pearl?'

'How about you stop talking nonsense and I have another go at kissing you?' growled Ethan.

He didn't wait for her reply, because she was looking up at him with the answer in her eyes.

We do hope that you have enjoyed reading this large print book.

Did you know that all of our titles are available for purchase?

We publish a wide range of high quality large print books including:
Romances, Mysteries, Classics
General Fiction
Non Fiction and Westerns

Special interest titles available in large print are:
The Little Oxford Dictionary
Music Book, Song Book
Hymn Book, Service Book

Also available from us courtesy of Oxford University Press:
Young Readers' Dictionary
(large print edition)
Young Readers' Thesaurus
(large print edition)

For further information or a free brochure, please contact us at:
Ulverscroft Large Print Books Ltd.,
The Green, Bradgate Road, Anstey,
Leicester, LE7 7FU, England.
Tel: (00 44) **0116 236 4325**
Fax: (00 44) **0116 234 0205**

JUST A MEMORY AWAY

Moyra Tarling

In hospital, Alison Montgomery cannot remember her own name. She hears the doctors' hushed whispers — sees their worried glances, which speak of the dark secrets lying just beyond the locked shutters of her memory. Then they bring her the stranger who says he's her husband. But why can't she remember loving a man as compelling as Nicholas Montgomery? And yet the shadows in his eyes clearly reveal that there's something in their past better left forgotten . . .

SECRETS IN THE SAND

Jane Retallick

When Sarah Daniels moves to a sleepy Cornish village her neighbour, local handyman and champion surfer, Ben Trelawny is intrigued. He falls in love with her stunning looks and quirky ways — but who is this woman? Why does she lock herself in her cottage — and why she is so guarded? When Ben finally gets past Sarah's barriers, a national newspaper reporter arrives in the village. Sarah disappears, making a decision that puts her life and future in jeopardy.